D1522879

TWO FOR ONE

Center Point
Large Print

Also by Barry Day and available from
Center Point Large Print:

Sherlock Holmes Novels:
 The Shakespeare Globe Murders
 The Alice in Wonderland Murders
 The Copycat Murders
 The Apocalypse Murders
 The Seven Deadly Sins Murders

**This Large Print Book carries the
Seal of Approval of N.A.V.H.**

TWO FOR ONE

A Sherlock Holmes/ Jack Watson Novel

Barry Day

CENTER POINT LARGE PRINT
THORNDIKE, MAINE

This Center Point Large Print edition
is published in the year 2017 by arrangement with
Mysterious Press/Open Road Integrated Media.

The text of this Large Print edition is unabridged.
In other aspects, this book may vary
from the original edition.
Printed in the United States of America
on permanent paper.
Set in 16-point Times New Roman type.

ISBN: 978-1-68324-540-7

Library of Congress Cataloging-in-Publication Data

Names: Day, Barry, author.
Title: Two for one : a Sherlock Holmes/Jack Watson novel / Barry Day.
Description: Large print edition. | Thorndike, Maine :
  Center Point Large Print, 2017.
Identifiers: LCCN 2017032736 | ISBN 9781683245407
  (hardcover : alk. paper)
Subjects: LCSH: Holmes, Sherlock—Fiction. | Watson, John H.
  (Fictitious character)—Fiction. | Large type books. | GSAFD:
  Mystery fiction.
Classification: LCC PR6054.A928 T86 2017 | DDC 823/.914—dc23
LC record available at https://lccn.loc.gov/2017032736

For LYNNE and COCO
. . . who both see *and* observe

TWO FOR ONE

ONE

Perhaps I should begin by telling you how I came to meet Sherlock Holmes.

I'd been involved in one of those boring bread-and-butter cases that usually end up as bread-and-margarine and low fat margarine at that. You don't expect much to start out with and that's exactly what you end up with. Stale, flat and most definitely unprofitable, as the Bard says.

Oh, there was one bonus. As I was pointing out to this errant husband the desirability of returning to the domestic hearth and home—his forsaken spouse being my client of record—the lady who was the current object of his affections decided to strike while the iron was hot and used that very item to register her personal displeasure.

As all the best private eye novels have it—a bottomless black pool opened at my feet and I dived in.

When I finally surfaced, I was lying propped up in a hospital bed, bandaged like the *Curse of the Mummy's Tomb* and Sherlock Holmes was sitting in a chair at the corner of the room.

Well, he was and he wasn't.

I could see him but when I looked directly at him, I could also see *through* him. It was as though he had decided to materialize and hadn't

9

quite finished the job. There was the Inverness cape and the close-fitting cap so familiar from the stories. There was the aquiline profile and the hooked meerschaum pipe. Then I remembered reading that Conan Doyle had never had Holmes smoke a meerschaum. At which point it morphed into a well-used briar, which didn't appear to surprise Holmes half as much as it did me, for he puffed on it contentedly.

Clearly, I was hallucinating and I shook my head to clear it. Which was a distinct mistake, as the contents of an average-sized junk shop rattled round inside it. When most of it had settled and I ventured to open my eyes again, Holmes was still there.

Now he was studying me intently and I gained the distinct impression I wasn't the only one in the room who wondered what the hell was going on—even though, strictly speaking, I was the only one in the room, if you see what I mean.

Then, even though his lips didn't move, Sherlock Holmes spoke inside my head.

"Well, Watson, this is a fine old kettle of fish. But apart from that rather rakish bandage you are sporting for some reason, I declare you look the same blithe boy as ever you did. If anything you look younger than I remember—though I must say, I miss the moustache."

As he spoke, the strangest sensation came over me.

For, you see, my name *is* Watson. Jack Watson. Licensed Private Investigator in the City of the Angels, Los Angeles. Forty years old, currently a bachelor of this parish and marginally solvent on a good day. Now that I've started, I might as well get the boring biographical bit out of the way. Born in Cleveland. Well, everybody's got to be born *somewhere* and it *could* have been New Jersey. Quite bright at school and might easily have amounted to something if I hadn't cottoned on to the fact that flunking was more fun than competing. Even so, I finished up at UCLA. Minored in English Lit. Majored in movies, my lifelong passion. Well, I was in the right town for it. And that's quite enough about me for now.

So, there I am, Jack Watson, minding my own business—and having it minded for me by a lady with a steam iron.

And now, for some reason I couldn't begin to fathom, a fictional character seems to think—through a coincidence of name—that I was *his* Watson.

So how do you resolve a situation that doesn't really exist to begin with?

Hey, you're a private eye, Watson. Go figure.

"Come, old fellow, it's not like you to lie abed when the game's afoot. Stir your stumps!"

And with that Holmes drifted out of the chair he had been approximately occupying and began to hover near the door. For no good reason other

11

than reflex action I found myself struggling into my street clothes and then navigating the hospital corridors towards the reception area.

After a brief exchange of opinions with the nurse on duty about the medical advisability of my releasing myself from their care and a rather more prolonged debate—in which she showed far more interest—about the validity of my credit card, I found myself in the parking lot and unlocking a Corvette (c.1967) the Smithsonian would kill for and I can barely pay for.

We were soon hiccupping our way—an imperturbable Holmes in the passenger seat—towards my apartment, a few unfashionable blocks behind Hollywood and Vine. I slid a tape of vintage rock 'n roll into the deck. I find it cancels out the vintage knock of the muffler. I'm definitely getting that muffler fixed when I get a case that pays its bills in anything but Confederate dollars.

Holmes seemed to quite like it. I noticed those long, thin fingers tapping out the rhythm on the dashboard.

A few minutes later we were pulling into the car port that serves as my garage.

I live in the upstairs half of a weathered clapboard that you could call retro, except that it's been this way all along. Some people might say the paint-work is peeling. I prefer to call it multi-textured. As for the strip of garden that holds the encroaching concrete at bay—well, I can honestly say that I've been into organic long before it was fashionable. Some of those weeds have been with me man and boy.

I tip-toed past the front door of the ground floor apartment but my fairylike tread failed once again and, turtle-like, my neighbor's head popped out.

Mr. Gryppe must be ninety, if he's a day, and I swear he never sleeps. Whatever hour of the night or day my benighted profession unloads me on that little wooden hill, Mr. Gryppe is there to give me a local news update. Insomnia was probably a prerequisite of his old occupation of undertaker. You can't afford to sleep in case you miss the latest customer for The Big Sleep. In idle moments I have imagined his advertising. "Our caskets undercut the competition. Gryppe Never Gyps!" But then, I have that pointless kind of imagination.

Today's bulletin was terse and to the point.

"He's been at it again. I told him." Then the head snapped back and the door was closed.

Holmes raised an eloquent eyebrow and drifted up the stairs. I clumped up after him, the point of my thoughtful tip-toeing having once again been lost.

I turned the key in the lock, edged the door open and, wraithlike, sidled in. Also in vain.

13

Mike leapt at me and gave me a big wet kiss.

Another world of explanation needed here, I think.

Mike is my dog. He's a cross between a Jack Russell and a Jack-of-all-Breeds. The first time I met him he was licking his privates. "Why do dogs do that?" I asked him. "Because they can, I suppose?" I answered myself after he'd paused to give it a moment's thought, then returned to his more imperative activity.

He was sitting on the landing outside my apartment door when I opened it one morning. His mission accomplished, he trotted in, established himself on the settee and has never left, except to accompany me wherever I go. There's a regular battle to see if I can close the front door before he can get out of it and it's another one I rarely win. On the rare occasions that I do, Mike will proceed to be "at it" until I return, thus earning Mr. Gryppe's commentary.

While I was disentangling myself, Holmes sat down in my favorite chair and stretched out his long arms and legs towards an imaginary fire. A moment later Mike was curled up at his feet and I had the distinct impression that each was perfectly aware of the other and just as much at home. Dogs! Now I had two uninvited lodgers.

I got myself a cold beer from the refrigerator and pointedly didn't offer one to either of the others. Since the only other chair was temporarily vacant, I lowered myself gratefully onto it and there we were, the three of us, staring at each other. So now what?

It was Holmes who broke the silence.

"A far cry from Baker Street, eh, old fellow? No peasoupers, no hansoms, no Mrs. Hudson, not even our old friend Lestrade. And even *I* appear to be in some way a figment of your somewhat fevered imagination. All we have to rely on— as ever—are our own resources and, of course, Mike here, the Hound of the Baskervilles . . ."

And at that I would swear Mike grinned. He certainly tried to rub himself against Holmes's legs and seemed surprised when they offered no resistance and he fell over.

"Nonetheless," he continued, "this new set of digs offers certain points of interest. Not to mention your funereal neighbor downstairs . . ."

"And what can you tell me about him, Holmes?" I found myself saying, as if by long habit.

"Other than that he was the proprietor of a funeral parlor for many years, once affected a wig, which he has ceased to wear, is hopelessly myopic but too vain to wear his spectacles for even the most casual social encounter and requires the services of a reputable dentist, I can tell you nothing. Oh, and he has a macaw of which he is inordinately fond."

Seeing my predictable astonishment, he elucidated.

"At first glance I thought he might be an actor. The complexion is that of a man who is used to wearing makeup and the wig . . . But the facial lines suggest a single assumed expression, that of a Uriah Heep–like servility. And who would need to be permanently welcoming but someone who was accustomed to welcoming people professionally without necessarily knowing them? The myopia? Observe the deep indentations on either side of the nose and the unfocused look. Even in his anger he failed to see you clearly.

"As for the dentistry . . . the human frame shrinks with age and dentures, which were clearly a considerable financial investment when he was a younger man, no longer fit his mouth properly, causing him to constantly push them back into place with his tongue . . ."

"But the macaw?" I interrupted. "I have never heard so much as a peep out of it?"

"That is because he keeps a cloth over the cage when he hears you about. I was able to catch a glimpse of a shrouded object over his shoulder as we passed. When his sole intention is to complain about your shortcomings, he has no intention of providing you with grounds for counter-complaint. Hence the silence of the bird. What put the matter beyond doubt was the feather adhering to the side of his head. He likes to perch the creature on his shoulder. And, of course, the residue on his collar, which I had initially thought to be dandruff . . ."

"Yes, Holmes," I said, "I get the picture."

"Your vocabulary seems to have deteriorated in my absence, my dear chap, if you don't mind my saying so. 'Get the picture,' for instance. And some of the argot you exchanged with the young lady at the hospital would not have passed your lips in the old days. Ah, well—*autres temps, autres moeurs*, I presume. Was it not our old friend, Oscar Wilde, who said that America hadn't been discovered—merely

"And now, shouldn't we be addressing ourselves to your new latest case?"

"Chance would be a fine thing," I muttered, draining my beer and wondering if I should forage for another. "I haven't had a sniff of a decent case for weeks. I'm thinking of entering my office for the World Dustball Championship."

Holmes appeared to be looking into the far distance as he said—"I think you'll find, Watson, that a client is en route for that very spot even as we speak. If you wish to remove those dustballs before he arrives, I recommend we take ourselves there post haste. Something else to do with a bird—or I miss my guess."

Minutes later the three of us were bowling along in the nearest approximation to a hansom cab I could muster (courtesy of General Motors).

17

TWO

The sky had that slightly smudged purple look, like the skin under the eyes of a woman who's been crying too long. The funny thing is, I'd never given Mother Nature a second thought until I became a private eye but these days, wherever I went, laconic imagery seemed to seep out of me. Too much Marlowe, I guess— Philip not Kit.

I tried it on Holmes for size but he and Mike just looked at each other, so I let it lie. Wordsworth might have done better with his observations on daffodils but I doubt it.

Fifteen minutes later we were parking outside my office building. I say "my" but in reality it was an "our" since I shared it with a mixed bag of other denizens.

There was Sharkey, the aptly-named bond bail man.

There was Goble, Gable and Gunst, a firm of cut price lawyers who looked as if, should business be slack, they would probably sue one another.

Down the corridor from me was the Colossal Casting Agency, a name presumably derived from the ladies of varying ages but uniformly impressive body mass who stomped their spike-heeled beat to and from the erratic elevator and never seemed to surface in any movie I ever watched, no matter how late the hour.

Whenever Bernie (Mr. Colossal Casting) and I ran into each other in the corridor, the routine was invariable—

"How's business?" Me.

"Colossal!" Him.

Then *he'd* say—"How's the private eye business?"

And *I'd* say—"Looking up."

It was the kind of routine that has made vaudeville what it is today.

As for the rest, their closed doors were a closed book to me. Behind them Tolstoy, Jr., might be tapping out *War and Peace 2* or aliens working on new plots for *The X-Files*. Who knew? Whatever it takes to make a buck. Right?

As we shed the Corvette, I saw Holmes inspecting the building—a sort of Nouveau-Deco-Rococo-Palazzo-Retro structure.

"It's called The Century Building," I said, to keep the conversation flowing.

"So I see. I was merely wondering *which* century would care to take credit for it?"

Inside the lobby there was the homey smell of chlorine that accompanied Mrs. Plack, our *hausfrau-in-residence* the way that other women trail clouds of Chanel No. 5. Mrs. P. regarded The Century Building the way other people viewed the Forth Bridge. The moment she'd finished cleaning it, it was time to start over.

"Who's a lovely boy, then?" she crooned, looking up momentarily from her bucket and mop. One glance at my bandaged head in her high gloss floor reassured me that she was addressing Mike.

Now, ordinarily Mike is his own man following the sound of his own drum but around Mrs. P. his cuteness is disgustingly Disneyesque. He even deigned to bend his head to be patted.

It was only after witnessing many such stomach-turning displays that I solved the puzzle. With an act of prestidigitation worthy of Maskelyne & Devant, Mrs. P. was able to transfer scraps she had secreted in her apron pocket, heaven knew how long before, to her patting hand and for Mike to effect the transfer from hand to mouth, so to speak, without a flicker of expression on either side to give the game away.

Some detective, huh?

To distract me further, she now addressed me through Holmes's ectoplasmic presence—

"You want me to clean your office?"

This was another regular routine that brightened up a dull day—at least it did for me.

"Dear lady," I say, giving my incredible impersonation of W. C. Fields, "Why, in my office there is dust . . ."

". . . that properly belongs in the Smithsonian."

Why do so many straight men feel the need to step on one's lines?

"So that's a No?"

"A definitely tentative 'No,' dear lady. Tell me, is there any part of my 'No' you don't understand?"

I couldn't imagine what Holmes was making of all this but the social niceties must be observed.

Like any woman, Mrs. P. must have the last word.

"Personally, I wouldn't want a visitor of mine ruining a beautiful new suit on a dirty chair but *chacun à son goût*."

"A *visitor?*"

"Yeah, and from what I can see you don't get that many that you can afford to waste a live one. Went up in the Death Trap . . ."—she indicated the antique elevator that stood with its mouth open, leering at us like a Great White at feeding time.

"Couple of ticks before you arrived. Well set up, good looking young guy. I'll have him when you've finished with him. But not as beautiful as you, my darling!"

Once again, I was relieved to find she was addressing Mike who, knowing when his performance had peaked and there were no more encores in the offing, was padding up the stairs. One ride in the Death Trap was enough for him. Except *in extremis*, it was plenty for me, too.

Holmes levitated and I hauled myself up the stairs in close pursuit. I thought I might have heard the Death Trap sigh but then, the isle is full of noises.

I certainly heard Holmes murmur something like—

"Deliciously Dickensian."

As I lumbered like Frankenstein's Monster towards my office door, I could see Holmes examining the legend inscribed there—

J.W.
P.I.

To begin with I'd had—

SPADE & ARCHER
J. H. Watson (Prop.)

But when prospective clients had insisted on seeing either Mr. Spade or Mr. Archer, I gave up. Whatever happened to good old-fashioned irony? Doesn't anybody watch old movies any more? Or read Dashiell Hammett, come to that?

Not that I'm having too much more luck with the latest incarnation. Troy, the ex-wrestler who acts as janitor for The Century (and who, I'm convinced, has something going with Mrs. P.) took one look at it and apologized to me most profusely. Clearly, vandals had stolen some of

23

the letters and it would be his pleasure to replace them for me, if I'd tell him what it was supposed to say.

At the moment the later afternoon sunlight gave it a rather dimensional 20th Century Fox logotype look, on account of the office door was ajar.

Slipping my trusty vintage Smith & Wesson .38 five shot from its shoulder holster, I motioned the others to stand aside. Though why an intruder thoughtless enough to leave the door open would want to shoot a dog, let alone an invisible man, wasn't quite clear to me.

I sidled around the door frame in the approved shamus manner and found myself facing a heavy set young man in a gleaming white silk suit, perched precariously on my sole visitor's chair.

It's not what you might call a welcoming chair at the best of times, I freely admit. I picked it up when the two lesbian lawyers next door split up and split and somehow I've never quite got around to fixing the gammy leg.

Nonetheless, my visitor was exacerbating the situation somewhat. He was trying to save his virgin suit by spreading his handkerchief on the seat and then hovering over it, like a maiden lady in a public lavatory, touching it at as few points as possible. It was neither a comfortable or comforting sight.

I probably made it even less so by stretching out

my hand—the one without the Smith & Wesson in it—in greeting. White Suit stood up gratefully, inspected my mitt briefly—presumably for additional dust—then shook it.

You can tell a lot about a man from his handshake—I'm sure Holmes has written a short monograph on the subject—and I could tell this man was nervous and that his nervousness extended beyond the size of his dry cleaner's bill.

Some of it I put down to the fact that Mike was now nosing his crotch, which I find scarcely ever puts strangers at their social ease. But it was more than that. This man did not relish his mission here today.

I motioned to Holmes to stand close to him and monitor his reactions, then turned the head gesture into a momentary discomfort with my bandages. It doesn't inspire confidence in the average client to see you addressing thin air.

"The door was open," said White Suit—which didn't surprise me owing to the tinny nature of the lock—"and the cleaning lady said to make myself at home."

Which didn't surprise me, either. Mrs. P. seemed to see The Century as her personal salon. I'd once addressed her as "our own Madame de Stael" but it hadn't really registered, I felt.

"Care for a drink?" I asked, pulling the office bottle of scotch with its mandatory two fingers of liquor from my bottom drawer, where it nestled next to nothing. I always keep it at the two finger lever, even it means adding water during lean times. I fished out two shot glasses from another drawer to keep it company and wiped them clean of fingerprints.

White Suit took a quick look at the glasses and shook his head.

"Not when I'm on duty, thanks."

I tried to turn the cap with my teeth, before realizing it would be a whole lot easier to pour if I were to put the gun down first. So I did and propped my feet on the desk instead. Now I was ready for business.

I took a slug of scotch-tainted water.

"So what can I do for you?" I asked. Then, with a sneaky look at Holmes, I added—"I beg you omit no detail, however apparently trivial it may appear."

I thought Holmes nodded his approval.

White Suit moved nervously over to the window and made as if to pull back the curtain. He thought better of it and wiped his hands on his handkerchief instead. Then he leaned over my desk and spoke so quietly that only I could hear. He was probably right. Mike has a loose lip.

"Mr. Watson, I'm here on a matter of great sensitivity that involves my employer."

"And your employer is . . . ?"

"Mr. Osgood Kane, the noted philanthropist

and recluse. He has lost something of great value to him and he wishes you to retrieve it.""

"A pearl of great price, I presume?" I mused. Now, be fair, how many private eyes throw in biblical quotations with a cut price daily rate?

"Not a pearl, Mr. Watson, but certainly an object of great price. By the way, may I introduce myself? My name is Perlman—Brent Perlman—and I am Mr. Kane's personal assistant."

Kane's name rang a loud bell right away. At one time he was a man who bestrode the Hollywood scene like a—whatever it is that bestrides things. His name was spoken in the same breath as those of William Randolph Hearst or Howard Hughes and with about as much affection. Fear was what Kane generated—fear and money.

He'd appeared out of nowhere—in the late 1940s, it would have been. Word had it that he'd made his money back east but nobody on this side of the land mass knew or cared what happened back east. Most of them would have a hard time finding it on a map. All they knew was Kane was soon a meal ticket, if you didn't mind eating his kind of food. And there were always a lot of hungry mouths in Tinsel Town.

He dabbled in independent productions for a while—C-picture Westerns and the kind of thrillers where the wall of the set shakes when somebody closes a door. Having cut his baby teeth on that, then he really splashed out. Bought one of the smaller studios, revamped it, then traded it in for a major, then two. Money was no object. And in any case, these were the golden years in Hollywood for the studio system. Movies poured off the production line like sausages and baloney was as good a description as any for most of them. Anything that could put sixty to ninety minutes between the title sequence and "The End" made money.

Kane made money and he made stars—literally. Remember how he took Phyllis Guggenhaft, a waitress from the Bronx, raised her hairline, re-shaped her boobs and chiseled her nose a tad and gave the world Alana Kidd? There were half a dozen more and most of them apparently ended up in his bed—though only the girls, as far as we knew. He supposedly even married one or two of them, if only for the look of the thing.

He saw television coming when everyone else was pooh-poohing it as a toy. Made several more fortunes from that and still was—without lifting a muscle. By now there probably weren't many muscles Osgood Kane *could* lift, for the man must be in is mid to late eighties. Nonetheless, the money was still there and the aura of power was still there. You didn't screw with Kane, unless you wanted to risk getting terminally screwed yourself. That was the man who wanted to see me.

Was the challenge of the chase coursing

through my veins? Not unless it felt like cold running water in a walk-up. Did we need the money? That was an easier one to answer.

"I'll be happy to help Mr. Kane," I said in my smoothest Nick Charles manner. If I'd had a small, neat William Powell moustache, I'd have stroked it. "My fee is a hundred . . ." I saw Holmes wag an admonitory finger—"and fifty a day plus expenses." Holmes seemed to expect something more. "My fee is unvarying, except when I choose to waive it altogether. And on this occasion," I added swiftly, "I do not choose to waive it." Holmes almost smiled.

I realized that much of my performance—which was impressing the hell out of me and even seemed to satisfy Holmes—was lost on White Suit, since he was busily writing out a check on his knee. He tore it out, waved it dry, then let it float down on to my desk.

"Here is one thousand dollars as a down payment, Mr. Watson. You will find my employer not ungenerous, as long as you perform your duties to his satisfaction. Here is our address . . ." He flipped a card from an inside pocket, like a magician producing a dove, and it landed on top of the check.

"Shall we say tomorrow morning at ten?"

"By all means. I'll say it right now. 'Tomorrow morning at ten.' "

"Good evening, Mr. Watson. Let us hope this is

the beginning of a beautiful friendship. *A demain*, as our French friends say."

He looked comfortable for the first time since I had entered the room—most certainly because he was leaving it.

"A little bird tells me it may well be," I replied for some reason.

He turned at the door and the comfort had all drained away. He seemed about to say something, then thought better of it.

The door closed behind him and this time the lock held.

I was about to put my feet back on my desk when Holmes hissed—

"Watson, how many times must I tell you that the interview is not over merely because the client has left the room? The window, man—the *window!*"

I got there just in time to see Perlman approach an open top Porsche parked just outside the building. He vaulted—rather self-consciously, I thought—into the driver's seat, looking at his passenger for a reaction.

All I could see from above was a large white straw hat and the long sleeved arm of a white chiffony dress draped over the back of the driver's seat. Around the wrist was a gold bracelet of some intricate intertwined design.

Then she must have said something to Perlman,

for his rather simpering expression vanished and he turned the key in the ignition. A moment later the car roared away, burning rubber and spraying dust all over Mrs. Plack's newly-washed lobby. But then, what's the point of driving a Porsche, if you don't burn rubber and spray dust?

I turned to find Holmes peering over my shoulder. It's unnerving to have an insubstantial presence anywhere in your line of vision but particularly so when you're nose to nose.

"Nice wheels," I offered. "Cool chick," I added.

"If you mean the motor vehicle the young man was driving, I defer to your judgment, Watson. I am no authority on these matters. And if you are using contemporary vernacular to refer to his lady companion, I defer even more. The fair sex—as I have often remarked—is your department. Unless I miss my guess, the motor car is her property—and so is he. I must say, I would not be happy to entrust so obviously expensive an item to one in his condition . . ."

"In what condition?"

"Come, old fellow. Surely you saw the fellow's contracted pupils, noticed the way he continually wiped his nose, although he was clearly not suffering from a cold? No, he is obviously an habitue of some substance, almost certainly cocaine. A six and a half or possibly a seven per cent solution, at a guess. Or more likely inhaled. You of all people should know that I have a certain—shall we say—expertise in these matters.

"He indubitably came here to deliver his master's invitation but the lady is most definitely part of the plot.

"And now, Watson, let me be your medical advisor for once. Time for you to take a rest after your eventful day. An early night will work wonders but first a little something nourishing. I only wish I could join you but something tells me that may be beyond even my powers. However, I shall join you vicariously. In spirit, as it were. Our old watering hole, Simpsons-in-the-Strand, alas, does not appear to be an option but I did notice one establishment on our way here that seemed to be drawing the passing trade. The Cheeky Chicken, I believe it was called. Or perhaps you would prefer 'chick.' Ah, I see friend Mike approves of the choice. I suggest we take ourselves there forthwith . . .

"Incidentally, I'm sorry to see you have given up your old service revolver. That Webley No. 2 saw us through many a scrape and I fancy we may miss its comforting presence. But we shall see. We shall see."

THREE

"You have heard me say, Watson—to the point of tedium, I do not doubt—that when you have eliminated the impossible, whatever is left, however improbable, must be the truth. The dilemma that faces us in this instance, old friend, is that it appears to be impossible to eliminate the impossible.

"Logic tells us that I should not be here and yet, patently I am—at least in part. And that part I, for one, find most welcome. It is good to see you again, Watson and, who knows, perhaps those powers that command our fates have one more case for us to solve before they intervene once more."

"Amen to that good wish, Holmes," I rejoined. Jesus, he'd got me talking like him now!

It was just before ten the following morning and we were sailing smoothly through the Hollywood Hills. The sun was giving us a full frontal smile that would put Carol Channing to shame and even the old Corvette was chugging along, as if she'd had a double dose of Geritol. Maybe Holmes had put a hex on it.

I reflected on the previous day. After the Cheeky Chicken had done its worst—or, in Mike's case, its best, since he finished up eating most of it, including the wrappings—we'd returned to Fort Watson, pausing only briefly to make macaw noises when Mr. Gryppe popped his head out.

Frankly, the day *had* taken it out of me in more ways than one. A bop on the bean and a ghostly roommate are more than par for my particular course. I was only too happy to flop into my favorite armchair, compete with the assertive springs for my personal space and close my eyes for a few minutes.

Those few minutes turned into a good eight hours and when I came to I saw the morning sun back-lighting a snoring Mike on the settee opposite, giving him a totally unearned halo. It was only when I turned my head and saw Holmes hunched in the other armchair, his thin arms wrapped around his bony knees, that everything came flooding back.

Without quite opening my eyes, so that he wouldn't know I was awake yet, I studied him. For some reason I had the strangest sense of *déjà-vu*. I couldn't have been here before—and yet I *had* been here before, sitting companionably like this in silence, while Holmes pursued some abstruse mental problem through the reaches of the night.

"A three pipe problem, Holmes?" I heard myself say. For, indeed, he was smoking that battered briar, its smoke wreathing his head and yet, for some reason, I couldn't smell it.

"No, only two, old fellow. I am almost ashamed to say that I was revisiting those four cases that defeated me—three men and one woman. I have now seen the error of my methods as far as the men were concerned but I confess I remain baffled as to what I might have done differently about Irene Adler . . ."

"*The* woman?"

"*The* woman, as you say. But come, Watson, there is new work to be done and, if I may make a suggestion, we are likely to make more progress, if you will exchange your swaddling clothes for something less eye-catching. I think you will find a simple plaster will now suffice."

And, indeed, when I had unwound the bandage, a surprisingly small, though engagingly technicolored bruise met my eye and a manly Band-Aid—suggestive of a tavern brawl in defense of a lady's honor—did the job.

Pausing only to shower, change and refuel Mike, we were on our way to our date with destiny—and Osgood Kane.

We drove for a while in silence, as I pondered what Holmes had just said.

What seemed to be happening did defy logic but then, where had logic ever got me? A job that for some reason I enjoyed, even though it didn't pay well, when it paid at all, an apartment my late lamented mother would have considered one step down from a slum, a love life that came and went and that currently showed no sign of returning any time soon . . . and that was about the sum total of it.

On the other hand—as of right now—I had a partner I didn't have to pay that Philip Marlowe, Lew Archer and any other private eye you care to name would envy and a dog that was smarter than most people (and infinitely more supple in the hygiene department).

Looked at with that perspective, the streets we were passing through didn't look so mean after all. On top of that the sun was shining and we were off on the Yellow Brick Road to see the Wizard, the Wonderful Wizard of Osgood . . .

Kane Towers looked as if a baby giant had modeled Hearst Castle in playdough, then squashed it to fit a smaller space. Nobody—not even Osgood Kane—could buy the kind of acreage in the tone-y part of L.A. that William Randolph Hearst had sequestered for himself further up the coast at San Simeon back in the twenties. Kane had had to content himself with a drive that wound back on itself like a snake trying to scratch an itch.

"A long run for a short slide," I said, as we finally reached the front portico but only Mike seemed to appreciate the reference. Did they even have baseball in Holmes's time?

That giant kid had certainly liked turrets. They flourished like fungus on any surface that would hold them and pointed every which way. I'd have hated to have to clean that many windows—unless, of course, I was a professional window cleaner, which, from time to time I've considered as a more secure career path.

The place clearly made the same impression on Holmes. With the whisper of a smile he murmured—"This makes Baskerville Hall look like a Limehouse tenement, Watson. Furthermore, it might be said to give the phrase 'conspicuous wealth' a bad name. Shall we open the toy box?"

And, indeed, Holmes's imagery proved to be predictive, for when I gave the bell pull a tentative tug, we could hear a sequence of musical notes resound through the house.

"Ah," said Holmes, " 'The Ride of the Valkyrie.' So Mr. Kane is a fellow Wagner enthusiast. This encounter may prove interesting."

As the last notes died away and as if on cue, the great front door swung open to reveal a neat little oriental gentleman wearing servant's livery—black trousers, highly polished shoes and an immaculate white jacket. White seemed to be the color of choice in the Kane entourage.

In perfect unaccented English, which made me

wonder whether it was time for *me* to sign on with Berlitz, he said—

"Mr. Watson, I presume? The Master is expecting you. Please come this way. And do not worry about your companion—I will take good care of him."

It took me a moment to realize that he was referring to Mike and not Holmes. He said something to Mike in what I presumed was Chinese and I'll be damned if that mutt—who, as far as I know, has never been nearer to China than the bins outside a Chinese restaurant—didn't "sit and stay" by the door with a pathetically goofy smile on his face and watch as his master and reasonably reliable meal ticket receded down the marble hall.

I've always liked the word "eclectic" and I was using it for years before I looked up the meaning of it. Outside Kane Towers was simply late Gothic-Horrific. Inside it was Eclectic City. Suits of armor jostled with Impressionist paintings, Chinoiserie rubbed shoulders with Henry Moore on the one side and Tutankhamun's spare mummy case on the other. The whole thing deafened the eye and the one clear impression I was taking away was that there was a whole lot of moola lying around to be dusted in one shape or another. Once again, I found myself wondering whether Kane hadn't picked up the job lot at one of Hearst's tag sales.

By now we'd made so many turns and taken so many back doubles that I was thoroughly disoriented—if that's the word I want, considering who was doing the leading. It also occurred to me to wonder if, perhaps, that wasn't part of the point.

Although we didn't see another soul, I was aware that there was plenty of other life on the planet. From behind thick wooden doors came the buzz and hum of people and machines at work. I was pretty sure that, should the need arise, legions of support troops armed to the teeth would pop up like mushrooms—or possibly toadstools. The thought of toadstools armed to the teeth gave me a moment of childish pleasure.

Finally, Charlie Chan came to a halt in front of a pair of double doors that were made of clouded glass. It was then that I recognized the sound that had been getting steadily louder for the past several hours we had been walking.

You know how you can be aware of the sound of the sea for quite some distance before you catch sight of it? Then suddenly you do and all the pieces fall into place and you can relax.

Well, this wasn't the sound of the sea. This was the sound of all the birds in creation piping up at once.

"Welcome to The Aviary," said our oriental guide. "You will find Mr. Kane within."

And he opened one of the doors and stepped aside to allow me to enter.

Holmes and I moved into what was obviously an anteroom, for ahead of us was another pair of glass doors, misted on the inside. Even where we stood the temperature was significantly higher than the corridor outside and the condensation suggested the main room was even warmer but for the moment I could see nothing of what it contained.

Behind us there was a purposeful click. Mr. Chan was not going to accompany us any further. I just hoped he'd left a road map on the door handle, so that we could find the front door and the real world again.

Holmes was now at the far door and I had the distinct impression that it was only the inconvenience of my corporeal presence that prevented him from walking straight through it. But then patience had never been Holmes's strong suit, I said to myself. And then I asked—but how do you know that?

Crossing mental fingers, I opened the door.

The sight that met my eyes is hard to describe unless, like me, you were brought up on a diet of boys' adventure stories and hokey science fiction films. The closest I can come to it is to say that it was how Conan Doyle's Professor Challenger must have felt when he finally got a look at that Lost World.

There were birds, birds . . . and then more birds. There were birds cawing, screeching and whistling on every surface in what I could discern as a virtual jungle of tropical trees and bushes. There were birds of every color of the rainbow and then some, most of them swooping and circling. There were even birds pottering about on the ground at our feet—though I noticed they gave Holmes a wide berth.

I stood there for a moment, wondering if I had somehow stepped into some state-of-the-art projection room and all of this was caused by special effects. At which same moment something plopped on my shoe. No, this was real, right enough.

"Over here, Mr. Watson." The voice was metallic, amplified. "Turn right at the sago palm in front of you. And don't mind my little friends. They can be a trifle playful at times but they mean no harm."

A tiny green and purple creature underlined his point by darting at me and nipping me painfully on the ankle. I side-footed it, squawking, into a nearby shrub. I was brought up to believe it isn't done to bite your guests, certainly not on the way in.

Sago palm—whatever that is—turn right . . . and there before me was a clearing in the jungle and in it, seated in a motorized wheelchair with a

41

small table at its side, was the biggest bird I had seen in the aviary so far.

Osgood Kane—for I recognized him immediately, even though the rare photographs one saw of him in the press had clearly been taken decades ago—had become, as so many of us are fated to do, the thing that he beheld. In extreme old age he had come to resemble the birds he so clearly adored.

The body imprisoned in the wheelchair was that of a living mummy, but it was the face that caught the eye. Mr. Gryppe had aged into a turtle but Kane had turned into a vulture. The nose was beaky and—as Shakespeare said of Falstaff— "sharp as a pen." The head was almost totally bald and the few remaining strands of white hair lay plastered flat against it, giving it a sleek appearance. The chin had disappeared into the wattles of creased skin on his neck.

Only the eyes were alive and the desiccation of the rest of him seemed to give them an unnatural brilliance. Bright and beady and missing nothing—including the mental evaluation I had just been making.

"Please take a seat, Mr. Watson. It was good of you to spare me the time in your busy schedule at such short notice."

If there was a touch of irony in his tone, it was lost by the distortion of the sound of what he said. And then I saw the explanation of that metallic quality in his speech. Osgood Kane's vocal chords had been removed. He was talking through a voice box. When he saw me looking, claw-like fingers fiddled with a small gadget on the side table.

"I must apologize for this inconvenient contrivance. When I wish to communicate with the rest of the world, I am forced to use it. Fortunately, I no longer wish to do so on anything but an intermittent basis. And, of course, I have the faithful Perlman to fetch, carry and occasionally bark for me. By the way, what did you do to him to make him so flustered yesterday? His fur was decidedly rubbed the wrong way.

"A delicate flower, Perlman . . ." The bright eyes were amused now. "He blows with the wind—and swings with it, too, I would guess. Though at this stage of the game even prurience loses its appeal. Always wears white, you know. Something symbolic there, don't you think?"

He laughed and the amplified sound reverberated around the room, causing the birds to rise in the air as one. The noise was deafening. When it had died down a little, Kane whispered as confidentially as a man in that condition can whisper.

"You know, he hates to come in here. He's afraid one of my little friends will do unto his precious white suit what one of them has just done unto yours!"

The shriveled hand went to the mouth as he enjoyed what was clearly one of his favorite jokes.

"Here," he pushed a box of tissues across the table towards me. "The dear creatures are no respecters of person. I suffer my own share of their little tributes. But look at them. Are they not worth a little trouble for so much beauty?"

I thought this might not be precisely the moment for too much truth, so I contented myself with using the tissues.

"No, Mr. Watson . . ." The playfulness was now over and it was time for the matter in hand, whatever that was. "That is what I like about birds. They are their own masters in all the ways that matter. Free spirits. Unfettered by the too, too solid earth that claims us all in due time. But enough of philosophy which—as Keats reminds us—can clip an angel's wings . . .

"I have called you here because I want you to find a bird for me."

"You don't feel you have enough?" I looked up—carefully.

"I want you to find a particular bird. *This* bird . . ."

His hand went to a small cloth-wrapped package on the table next to him. Slowly and methodically he unwrapped what was inside and handed it to me.

I found myself holding an exquisitely-carved

golden bird with its wings spread. It was about four inches across and about as long. And it was magnificent in every detail. It seemed poised as if about to take flight and at its feet were some wavy lines that might have been the artist's representation of the branches of a tree.

And the *eyes* . . . somehow the sculptor or the artist or whatever he was had managed to convey the sense that the bird was looking right at you. The red eyes were every bit as beady as their owner's but infinitely more malevolent.

And somehow the darned thing seemed to burn my hands. The heat in the room was close to unbearable but this was something more. I handed it back to Kane like a hot potato.

"The Borgia Bird, Mr. Watson—unique and irreplaceable."

"But you don't *need* to replace it—you have it already."

"Ah, if only . . . We collectors are strange birds—if you'll excuse the execrable pun, Mr. Watson. We want to own something unique and, if no one else in the world ever sees it again, it only adds to the pleasure. So we will squirrel it from the light of day, take it out occasionally at dark of night to gloat over it, then hide it away again. A form of madness, no doubt, but a well-documented one and divine madness, as I can attest. The Bird has been my own form of dementia these many years.

"But perhaps I should give you a little of its background, so that you will understand better what I seek and why.

"The Borgia Bird is so known in the world of antiques because it 'fell into the hands' of Cesaré Borgia around 1502. Which almost certainly means that whoever owned it at the time was summarily dispatched. Cesare gave it as a present to his sister, Lucrezia, with whom he was incestuously involved. After the dissolution of that feral but undoubtedly fascinating family the Bird's history is cloudy. Over the centuries it seems to have passed from hand to hand, usually leaving blood on those hands.

"Many years ago—at a time when I was myself living in Europe—it passed into mine and I have been its guardian ever since . . ."

"Until now?"

"Until now . . ." Kane seemed lost in his own thoughts. "It is an *objet* without price, Mr. Watson. Think of the things it has seen, the places it has been. Even to touch it is to share a little of all that."

Then he seemed to return to the present.

"I confess the Bird became something of an obsession with me—a conduit of sorts to other, more exotic worlds. As you see, I have become a prisoner in my own body." The clawed hand gestured towards the skeletal frame in its confining wheelchair.

"I dared not exhibit it for fear of theft, yet I could not bear to be without it. And then I had what seemed to me at the time a brilliant idea. I would have a replica made, so that I could have my bird and hide it, so to speak. I had come across a man who had provided me with the occasional little *objet* and he happened to be a superb craftsman. He also happened to be corrupt enough that money would buy both his talent and his silence.

"To cut to the chase, as you Americans are so fond of saying, this man made me my replica and it was a brilliant replica, as you may see . . ." He weighed the golden bird in his hand. "So the Bird went back to his secret nest and this bird shone by my side through the endless hours of an old man's day. A touching picture, is it not?"

"And then . . . ?"

"Every so often, when the mood would take me, I would have Perlman wheel me to where the nest was hidden. Naturally, I was careful not to let him see its precise location. Then I would commune with my little friend and we would relive great adventures together. You will, of course, have observed precisely what species of bird this is, Mr. Watson?"

He held it up for my inspection and for a moment the sunlight breaking through the roof of palm leaves seemed to set it on fire, so that it blinded me.

"A phoenix, Mr. Watson. The supreme bird of fable that springs forth in various cultures that are otherwise quite unrelated. The Egyptians claimed it. So did the Arabs, the Indians, even the Chinese in their time. It clearly symbolizes something fundamental in human nature."

Now my memory dredged up the reference.

"Isn't that the bird that's supposed to come out of the fire?"

"Correct. The phoenix lives its given span of years, as we all do, then it makes its nest, sings a melodious dirge—which, alas, few of us manage to do!—then flaps its wings to ignite the pyre and burns itself to ashes. And then the miracle occurs. The bird is reborn from the flames to start the cycle all over again. And perhaps that is the secret of its attraction. We would all like to be the phoenix—some of us more than others.

"But I fear an old man is wandering into the byways of philosophy. Yesterday I had Perlman take me to Shangri-La—only to find the Bird had flown . . . And that is why I have sent for you, Mr. Watson. Return my bird to me and you will find me a most grateful client. Now, what more do you need to know?"

"Who else lives here, Mr. Kane? Who else might have had access to the Bird?"

Out of the corner of my eye I saw Holmes nod his approval.

"Apart from my secretary and amanuensis,

Perlman, whom you met, there is Kai-Ling, my man servant, a fairly recent acquisition. It was he who conducted you here."

Charlie Chan. Right.

"There are the usual menials who come and go on a daily basis. Only Mrs. Chilvers, the housekeeper, lives in. And then, of course, there is my daughter, Nana. She is my only family . . ."

Then, as if anticipating my next question, he added—"I would rather you did not bother her. She has not been well and is easily upset. I have not told her the news yet. She will worry excessively on my behalf. We are very close. No, Mr. Watson, if you will take my advice, you will start your inquiries with the man who made me my replica. He has his ear to the ground— or should I say the underground. If someone is attempting to sell the Bird, Quentin Mallory will undoubtedly hear of it. Perlman can give you his address, as you leave.

"And now, Mr. Watson, I'm afraid all this talk has rather tired me. I am not normally so garrulous but catch a zealot on the topic of his religion and . . ." He gave a minimal shrug and what might have been a smile in my general direction.

Just behind him I saw Holmes nod, as if to say we had learned as much as we were likely to on this first interview.

I rose to my feet. Since Kane had both hands

occupied holding and stroking his clone bird, I didn't offer him mine. He seemed to have fallen back into his reverie but, as I moved back into the jungle, I heard him say—

"You may contact me at any time through Perlman, Mr. Watson, and he will take care of the usual arrangements. Since we cannot have Sherlock Holmes, I am trusting you to act *in loco parentis*. I wish you 'Good hunting!' "

Holmes and I now repeated the decontamination process in reverse. No sooner had the inner door of the antechamber hissed to behind us than the outer door swung back to reveal the inscrutable Kai-Ling. It was as if he had been monitoring my every move—which he probably had. With an inclination of the head he led me back by a quite different route, which only confirmed my suspicion that on the way in we had been given the runaround—or at least the walk-around—to soften me up for my meeting with his employer.

It was as well that on the return trip he appeared to have run out of either guile or patience, for two things happened that we might otherwise have missed. At the head of a small staircase hung a large portrait. Kai-Ling would have hurried me on but I insisted on stopping to study it and there was little he could do about it, short of being downright rude and the Chinese haven't yet figured out how to compete with the West in a way the West chooses to understand.

It was Holmes who gave me the idea, to be honest, when I saw him hovering around it. It was of a man in early middle age. He was standing in what was clearly hunting gear with a rifle over one shoulder. In the other hand he held a brace of dead game birds of some sort. The setting looked somehow European but the artist had provided no background clues to put it anywhere specific.

The man's face was handsome in an aquiline sort of way but the eyes had an unsettling expression in them and the mouth was a thin line turned down at the edges. You would not wish to meet him on a dark night unless you knew for sure that he was on your side and had a signed affidavit to prove it.

"So our friend was Herne the Hunter before he became St. Francis of Assisi?" I heard Holmes say. "Presumably a conversion on the road to some Damascus?" I was about to reply when I saw that Kai-Ling had fixed his gaze upon me.

I already had the impression that he had not formed too high an opinion of my capabilities and the sight of me talking to myself would do little to change that perception. It could wait until we were outside.

The second event occurred as we turned a corner into the entrance hall. Perhaps because we were returning by a different route, we took them by surprise but clearly the two people standing there hadn't heard us approach. A man and a woman were standing there, engaged in what I can only describe as a lively difference of opinion. To be brutally frank, she was giving him not merely a piece of her mind but most of it. He wasn't liking it one bit and he began liking it a lot less when he saw that we were witness to it.

The man was our old friend The Man in the White Suit and obviously not the same white suit since there was not a mote of dust to be seen within a mile. He could have posed for the "After" in a detergent commercial and cleaned up in more ways than one.

The lady was our old friend's old friend from yesterday. This I could deduce from the large floppy white straw hat she was wearing that once again shielded her face. Today she was wearing another floaty, pastel Laura Ashley number that also covered her from wrist to neck.

Perlman said something to her and she looked instinctively in our direction. I saw a beautiful sculpted face, the nose strong and straight, the mouth firm. But the thing I saw most was fear. It was the face of a frightened fawn. This woman was not just frightened to see me, a stranger in her home. She was frightened of much more. What with Perlman scooting off yesterday like the White Rabbit and now a nervous Nana, that made two in a row.

Before we could get any closer, she turned on her heel and disappeared into a nearby room, closing the door firmly behind her.

And good morning to you, Ms. Kane, I thought. For I was in little doubt that the Disappearing Frightened Lady was Nana Kane.

By the time we reached Perlman, he had recovered much of his composure and I had a good idea that he would die rather than lose it in front of the imperturbable Chinese.

It took only moments for him to scribble Mallory's address on a discreet business card with the assurance that his private number would find him at any time of the day or night. A firm manly handshake—a little too manly?—and we were at the front door where—will miracles never cease?—Mike was still sitting and staying. This dog, whose hindquarters never touch the floor long enough to warm it when he hears my command, had been sitting like Patience on a monument for the past hour. Now, on a word from a Chinese he had never laid eyes on in his life, he snaps out of it like a patient out of hypnosis and trots amiably to the car without even giving him the soulful eye that expects a treat. When I have more time Mike and I need a man-to-dog conversation about loyalty and priorities.

"Well, Holmes, what did you make of that?" We were driving back to the office and the architecture of Hollywood, which so often strikes me as being transplanted straight from a comic book, looked quaintly suburban after what we had just seen.

"As I'm sure you were well aware, the loquacious Mr. Kane told you precisely what he wanted you to hear—not a word more and not a word less. In fact, he told you so much with such apparent candor that you felt he had told you all. But the man is an actor, Watson. I would venture that he has been acting most of his life—perhaps even acting for his life on occasion. He is no more Osgood Kane than I am—Charlie Peace or Benjamin Disraeli . . ."

"Then who *is* he?"

"That, I expect, will emerge in due course and may well be the key to much else. At this moment *anno domini* has restricted his range but it would be rash in the extreme to accept him as the foolish fond old man he presented to you just now. He may sit in a veritable aviary but, in reality, a closer analogy would be the spider in the middle of his web. His physical movements may be limited but his reach is unimpaired and, like the spider, he feels every tiny vibration when someone touches his web.

"The key to the future invariably lies in the past, old fellow. Something about the portrait is important but I am not sure what. What was it Hamlet said to Gertrude when he made the comparison between the portraits of his father and uncle? 'Look now upon this picture and on this—the counterfeit presentment of two brothers.' We have just observed the counterfeit presentment of two Kanes. And there may be more. Oh, Watson, if only this were Baker Street, I would have my Day Books, my files. The answer would lie there . . ."

It was that remark that prompted me to say—a trifle defensively, I fear—"I may not have Day Books, as you call them, but I have something just as encyclopaedic."

"And that is?"

"Morrie Saks."

I'd known Morrie for donkey's years. Christ, everybody had known Morrie for donkey's years. Morrie was a Hollywood institution just as much as Grauman's Chinese Theater used to be or the MGM lion—though Morrie's bite was considered a lot more lethal than the lion's bark.

Morrie was a gossip columnist who'd started when Winchell was in his prime and outlasted those two poisonous old biddies, Hedda and Louella. He turned his stuff into the *Los Angeles Sentinel* and it was syndicated just about everywhere. The acres of tropical rain forest that had been sacrificed to Morrie's morbid revelations didn't bear thinking about.

We met in a dingy bar round the corner from

the *Sentinel* offices—not from any reason of confidentiality but simply because the office, like just about everywhere in the free world these days, had a strict No Smoking policy and Morrie on a good day could compete with a Detroit chimney stack. Today was a good day.

When he'd coughed himself quiet, he paused to fire up one unlighted cigarette from its predecessor and then peered at me through the haze.

"So?" It was a typical Morrie cut-the-crap greeting.

I guess when he was young—somewhere back in prehistory—Maurice Saks must have been a fine upstanding specimen of a man but age had worked its sorcery and laid waste to what had once been. Now he was a gnome, liver-spotted and bald-pated except for a silvery fringe around the ears that looked as though it had been stuck on with a hung-over hand. Only the sharp black eyes gave the clue that anyone was home and, as many knew to their cost, they missed nothing. He and Kane had a lot in common and age had a lot to do with it.

I'd like to have suggested to Holmes that Morrie owed me one but it wouldn't have been strictly true. We all owed Morrie several and that was the way he liked it. That way he could always lean on us for favors. Morrie traded in information the way folks on Wall Street trade in pork belly futures or whatever.

"Osgood Kane," I said.

From the extra second he took to make sure his cigarette was alight, I could tell I had his serious attention.

"That's a pretty big rock you've just turned over, Jack. Lots of nasty, slithery things under a rock that size."

"Such as?"

"Over the years just about everything. Quite apart from the movies, Kane had a finger in just about every pie anybody baked. Usually through some intermediary or another, so that he could never be connected directly with anything shady. Investments, real estate, new ventures, you name it. If it went wrong, someone else carried the can. If it went really wrong, people tended to disappear. Mr. Kane is only interested in win-win situations.

"I got pretty close to some of that stuff over the years and it was pointed out to me more than once that it would be smart of me to butt out . . ."

"Which I doubt you did?" I suggested.

"No, I'm a stubborn old fart but, since I could never quite pin anything down, I guess they figured I was harmless. Then the years went by, as the darned things have a habit of doing—both for me and for Kane—and now we're both barely living legends in our different ways. Well, who gives a shit what two old relics did and when?"

"Except *you* do."

"Except I do. Darn right, I do—or I've spent my life doing diddley-squat. No, I'd like to see that old bastard get his comeuppance before they send him down below where he belongs."

"What can you tell me about his background, other than what I'll find in the clippings files?"

I'd almost forgotten about Holmes, who had lit up his pipe, presumably to keep Morrie company. Then he suddenly said—

"Ask him about Kane's wife."

"Kane's *wife!*" I said, just about managing to turn an exclamation into a question. Presumably Kane had *been* married, since he had a daughter, but I had no idea he was at the moment.

"Happened quite recently. Private ceremony at the house. No guests. No announcement. Linda Grace, née Karen Dorakis, sometime movie actress . . ."

Linda Grace! I could picture her now. Dark pageboy hair, pouty lips. A latter-day B-picture Linda Darnell, which is probably where some studio publicist got the name they stuck on her. Got all the Bette Davis and Joan Crawford bitch parts when those two *grandes dames* finally hung up their false eyelashes. Unfortunately for her, she got them just when the genre was going out of fashion. After that, some television series that petered out without benefit of syndication. And after that—Osgood Kane, Meal Ticket, or so it appeared. Well, well, well. Now, why hadn't Kane thought fit to mention her?

Morrie Saks was now under full sail. Kane was clearly mother lode to him, if I may be allowed a mixed metaphor. The personal computer he had for a brain was spitting out bits and bytes or whatever computers spit out.

"Linda's been after him or someone like him for years. She's done the Mendelssohn mazurka more times than you've had hot dinners but none of them paid out worth a bent nickel. Even this one don't look so hot. I hear Kane's got her tied up with a prenup hand, foot, finger and fanny. He can dump her any time at a discount but, if she leaves him—zip, zilch . . ."

"So she's the n-th Mrs. Kane?"

"Surprisingly, she's not. Despite all the rumors—only the second, in fact."

"What happened to the first Mrs. K.? I suppose she took him to the cleaners?"

"No, because he sent her to the funny farm— and then he divorced her. Turned even *my* stomach. Kane married her in the late 1960s. He must have been around fifty at the time. She was in her early twenties, a society girl, quite a looker. Eloise Something-or-other . . ."

He was off on a mental trip down the years now, so I just let him roll.

"What he wanted was an instant dynasty and when she couldn't oblige right away, the Robber

Bridegroom was gone and the Wicked Baron appeared. When she finally did give birth a few years later, it was twins—a girl and a boy. The boy was never seen in public. The word was that Kane found the child below his expectations for a son and heir and had him adopted. The girl, Nana, he kept . . ."

"And the wife?"

"The birth was troublesome, the woman had lived under stress for years. She had a breakdown, became almost catatonic. Kane had her committed and, since she was of no further use to him as a Mother of Dynasties, he eventually divorced her. That kind of money buys any kind of freedom. She's still in the asylum for which he pays all the bills, on condition they never release her. Since it's Osgood Kane—who's Chairman of the Board, would you believe who's asking nicely, chances are they won't."

Something Kane had said bobbed to the surface of my mind.

"Kane said something about living in Europe?"

"He also referred to 'you Americans,' " Holmes added.

Morrie paused to light another coffin nail from the last.

"Ah, now this is where things get *really* interesting."

He seemed surprised that I seemed surprised.

"Oh, that other stuff is standard soap.

Hollywood-Babylon 101. Happens all the time on a smaller, cut price scale. No, the real skinny on Kane is something I pieced together about twenty years ago but could never prove. One day I had a visit from a guy called Arie Weintraub."

"The Nazi hunter?"

"The very same. While he was looking for evidence on some top boys who'd got out while the going was good, he came across some references to one Otto Kreizer, who was bidding to be in their league, if the game had gone to the ninth inning. Pull the threads together and for Otto Kreizer read . . ."

"Osgood Kane."

"Give the man a cigar! I trawled it around for a while but even in a town where folks of my particular persuasion tend to litter the ground like the leaves that strow the brooks in Vallombrosa . . ."

He gave a sly grin at my expression.

"I've always had a soft spot for Milton. It kind of counterbalances some of the shit that I have to write to read somebody who can *really* use words. Anyway, as I was saying, even the Jewish population was tired of all this holocaust-schmolocaust. If you live in a town of fiction, fact can be awfully boring. So I got no takers on the story but I'm prepared to bet your bottom dollar it's kosher. Kane the Kraut. Fade to black."

"Weren't you afraid he might make *you* disappear, since he obviously had a soft spot for the now-you-see-it-now-you-don't routine?"

"To begin with I was shit scared. Then I figured, if I couldn't get anyone to listen to me, then Kane *knew* nobody wanted to listen, so he was perfectly safe. Right? Why bother taking me out, when these things . . ."—and he held up his death stick as an exhibit—"would do it for him any day? His tough luck that I'm a walking statistic, the exception that proves the rule. And now it's water under the bridge-work. But I'd still like to see the little fucker nailed."

We sat in silence for a moment while I digested all I'd just heard. Then Morrie glanced at the battered Timex that had clung to his wrist like a barnacle ever since I'd known him and never told the right time, as far as I was aware.

"*Tempus fugit*. Virgil, you ignorant asshole. Gypsy Rose must put away her crystal ball and return to the Augean stables, there to vilify and slander those who have dared to raise their heads from the slime. Now you owe me two. A father's blessing on your head, my boy . . ."

And with that he disentangled himself from the booth in which we were sitting, coughed loudly enough to silence the bar momentarily, and picked his way towards the door and the world outside.

Holmes and I stayed where we were. It was Holmes who spoke first.

" 'Curiouser and curiouser, said Alice.' A mad first wife out of Jane Eyre, a disinherited and disappeared son and heir . . . and one thought Victorian fiction was sensational enough."

"And don't forget the present Mrs. Kane," I chipped in. "Why on earth didn't Kane mention her? Surely she has to go on the list of suspects in the light of that prenuptial agreement?"

"I suspect he refrained from mentioning her because he considers her irrelevant to his overall plan. But I presume you were aware of her existence during our visit?"

"Come along, Holmes," I said testily in a voice I scarcely recognized as my own, "are you telling me you were?"

"I saw no more than you did, old fellow. The difference is that I also observed, which you clearly did not. There were two ladies' wraps and two purses on the hall table as we left. Apart from the fact that their styles were markedly different, suggesting the divergent tastes of two separate women, it has been my observation that a woman will put away her outer clothing when she changes it for another set. Conversely, a servant will put it away for her. Ergo, two women had recently entered the house, one of whom we briefly saw.

"And where to now, Watson?"

• • •

Where to now was back to the car to collect Mike and drive back to the office for a quiet think.

So what did we have?

I put my feet up on the desk. I find I do most of my best thinking that way. I'm pretty sure it's approved in the Gumshoe Guide. They also recommend tilting the fedora forward over the eyes but, since that would mean actually buying a fedora, I've persuaded myself that's not *de rigeur*. It is, after all, a very old edition that came with the office.

From this semi-recumbent posture I reviewed the situation with piercing analytical logic. We had . . .

. . . an ex-Nazi war criminal who got rid of people, including his own infant son, and who wanted me to retrieve a valuable antique bird that he had almost certainly obtained as war loot . . . an understandably neurotic daughter who seemed frightened of something, if only of her own shadow . . . a sexually ambiguous body-guard or whatever . . . and an Invisible Wife. An everyday story of Hollywood folk. Well, it was a start.

A couple more crazies and we could play Happy Dysfunctional Families.

I had come to this earth-shattering assessment and was reaching for the scotch-and-water drawer when there was a knock at the office door.

"Come," I said. Nero Wolfe would have said "Come."

And in came a small Chinese gentleman with one of those white jackets and paper caps they wear to deliver Chinese takeaway. Which was perfectly appropriate, since he happened to be delivering Chinese takeaway. The only problem was—I hadn't ordered any.

Muttering a guttural Chinese something or other, he dumped a brown paper bag on my desk and was gone.

There was a moment's silence while we all reacted in our individual ways. Holmes inspected the bag from all sides without actually touching it. Not that he could have, in all probability. Mike stood at the desk on his hind legs and gave it a good sniff, decided it wasn't worth the effort to be vertical and went back to his chair. I brought my mouth back to the Closed position.

My mother had a saying she quoted often. She claimed she got it from *her* mother which, I suppose, makes it something of a Watson family tradition. "What you don't know can't hurt you." Frankly, it's a thesis I've never subscribed to. I've frequently been hurt by people I've never laid eyes on before. I'd rather say—"What you don't open probably won't hurt you, all things being equal."

Holmes broke the deadlock.

"I think the odds are in favor of the package

being harmless, Watson. I suggest you open it and find what someone is clearly anxious for you to find."

The man's logic defied argument, so I did just that.

Inside, carefully wrapped in several layers of paper, was a single fortune cookie. Now, I have always had a strong aversion to fortune cookies, on account of the fact that I don't like the taste of stale cardboard, so I had no intention of eating it but I was most definitely intrigued to see what it said, if you see what I mean.

To smash it into smithereens was with me the work of a moment, nor was I laggardly when it came to picking up the piece of rice paper that lay coyly among the crumbs. I smoothed it out and took it over to the window to read what was on it.

A movement in the street below caught my eye.

"That's strange, Holmes," I said. "How the hell can they make any money if they deliver a single fortune cookie by limo?" For I had just seen the delivery man, now jacketless, hop into a black stretch limo with tinted windows that took off like a batmobile out of hell.

"Ah well," I said, "Elvis has left the building."

"I very much doubt that was his name, Watson. The man was clearly of Asian origin."

I decided not to pursue that matter.

"In any case, first things first, old fellow. What does the message say?"

"It says something in Chinese letters . . . Oh, yes, and on the back it says . . .

" 'WHAT WAS NOT EARNED
MUST BE RETURNED'
—Confucius (trans.)"

It was then that the phone rang. Being congenitally incapable of doing two things at the same time, I put the paper down, taking care to avoid Mike, who exercised a dog's prerogative to change his mind and was now licking up the cookie scraps and giving the desk a well-needed polish at the same time.

I picked up the phone and a man's voice said in an immaculate Oxford accent that I had heard somewhere recently—

"My dear Mr. Watson, I do apologize for serving you the dessert first but I have every hope that I shall not be required to serve you the main meal. It may prove less to your taste. You see, my friends and I are looking for a little bird that belongs to us and we have every hope that you will lead us to it. Rest assured that we shall monitor your every move. For instance, you should get the dog to lick the rest of the desk. That walnut veneer he is revealing is most becoming. *Au revoir*, Mr. Watson."

And there was a humming as he disconnected.

Instinctively I knew that Holmes had heard the conversation without needing to hear it.

Veneer, huh? The guy who sold it to me swore it was solid walnut. But I digress . . .

"The plot thickens, eh, Watson? Yes, this affair is certainly not without certain points of interest. You realize, of course, that your telephonic correspondent was the gentleman we were introduced to as Mr. Kai-Ling?"

The nickel dropped. Of course. It did occur to me to wonder why a man with a perfectly good day job should also run a Chinese restaurant but, then, these Chinese had the work ethic in spades. I decided to keep the thought to myself. In any case, it looked as though Kai-Ling had given up his day job.

"I don't know about you, old fellow, but I think I have had just about as much of modern living as I need for a while. What do you say we step back into the past and go and examine a few antiques? Ah, but wait a moment . . ."

As he spoke, Holmes had been instinctively drifting—and I use the world advisedly—over to the window. Frankly, I couldn't see much point in that. The Chinese waiter was long since gone and was probably sitting comfortably somewhere in front of a plate of American takeaway.

"Come over here, Watson. You appear to have another visitor . . ."

I joined him at the window and peered down at the familiar street below. The usual kaleidoscope of faces and figures moving like ants without a sense of purpose. But then I saw what must have caught his eye.

When the eddies in a stream move, they move in some sort of pattern and anything that does not have a pattern of its own stands out in relief. Among the eddies down below one figure was disturbing the flow by moving erratically to and fro, as if involved in some convoluted dance.

It was a young woman in her late twenties, who would take several determined paces towards our building, hesitate, then retreat a couple, as if she moved to a rhythm we could not hear.

"A client for you, old fellow, or I miss my guess. Her body language tells us all. She is anxious to communicate something, yet frightened of the consequences. It has taken most of her courage to come this far and she is now trying to summon up the rest. And, yes, she has done so . . ."

The woman disappeared from our view under the building's portico and I had barely time to arrange myself in my best casual-and-relaxed P.I. pose before there was a timid knock on the office door.

"Pray come in, madam." A little orotund, perhaps, but Jack Watson knows how to treat a lady.

The door inched open and in came—Nana Kane.

FOUR

And yet she was not the Nana Kane we had seen in the many mansions of her father's house.

That lady may have been scared and skittish but she had the kind of surface sophistication that could have stepped—and probably had—from the pages of *Vogue* or *Women's Wear Daily*.

This one had the same classic profile, the same long, aristocratic nose, the same full, predatory mouth—the same everything but seen in one of those distorting fairground mirrors. The pale blonde hair was pulled tight and taken up in a spinster's bun, the face was devoid of makeup and she wore a long gray cotton dress that almost met up with sensible flat shoes and gave no hint of a female shape beneath it. To cap it all, she had a pair of wire-framed glasses that clearly didn't quite fit, for she was constantly pushing them back up on her nose.

I felt my *sang froid* melting by the moment. What the hell was going on here?

"Aren't you going to ask the lady to sit down?" It was Holmes inside my head.

"Won't you take a seat, Miss Kane?" I said, dusting it down as I indicated the only chair she could possibly take.

She pulled back as though I had laid hands on

her—which, I assure you, I had not the slightest inclination to do. This was a fragile lady who might easily come to pieces in your hands.

"How do you know my name?"

Then the answer seemed to come to her and soothe her a little.

"Oh, but of course, you have seen my sister, Nana."

Sister?

She curtseyed into the chair as though afraid it might have lecherous designs on her.

"Mr. Watson—it *is* Mr. Watson, isn't it?—I'm afraid I am being most discourteous. I should introduce myself properly. My name is Anna Kane, though I choose not to use the name Kane. As far as I am concerned, that vile man does not exist for me. And I know I do not exist for him. Nor have I for a very long time.

"Nana told me you had been to see—*him*—and that is why I felt I must come and see you. You must help us, Mr. Watson. You must help *her!* I know my father is your client but there are things about him—about us—that you need to know before you go any further."

"Please calm yourself, Miss—please calm yourself, Anna," I said, summoning up my best bedside manner, as I tried to make head or tail of the situation.

"Mr. Kane told us—told me—that he had twins. A daughter, Nana, and a son who was adopted.

Now you're telling me there were *three* of you?"

"My mother nearly died giving birth to triplets, Mr. Watson. I'm told my father looked into the crib, decided that one little girl, Nana, was going to be a beauty but that my brother and I were runts in the litter and would have to go. In the Book of Life according to Kane only perfection is tolerated . . ."

The cleansing of the master race, I thought to myself.

"I was adopted and so, I believe, was my brother. I have never seen him—I never knew either of them existed—and I have no idea whether he is alive or dead. Nor, I'm sure, does Mr. Kane. I won't bore you with my history. Suffice it to say that I came back to this part of the world fairly recently and something inside me made me decide to find out about my origins. What I found sickened me, Mr. Watson. My life may have been dull but at least it has not been degraded like . . ."

"Like what?"

She swallowed hard and did not answer the question but I knew the information would not be long in coming. This, after all, was why she was here.

"I saw my sister's photograph in one of the society magazines. I made some inquiries that made sense of some of the things my foster parents had said that I didn't understand at the

73

time and quite suddenly the pieces fell into place. I knew then that I had to make contact.

"I waited for her one day outside ———" (she named a fashionable couturier) "She was shocked but intrigued, for she had no suspicion of my existence either. We went to a club she knew— Birdland—that belongs to a friend of hers and we had a drink. We must have looked a strange pair. You have seen us both now, Mr. Watson. Are we not two sides of the same coin?

"I didn't realize *how* different until she told me about her life. It sickened me, I tell you, sickened me! She has had all that tainted money can buy but the price she has had to pay! Our father began to sexually abuse her when she was very small and only stopped when he could no longer . . ."

She pulled out a bunch of crumpled tissues that had seen previous service and mopped her eyes. When she had controlled herself, she continued . . .

"When she was older and as beautiful as he had hoped she would be, she told me he would offer her to his special friends at dinner parties. Nothing was too degrading and she was expected to obey like a good little . . ."

"Nazi daughter," I completed the thought in my mind.

"Later came"—she paused, as if editing her thoughts—"oh, it is monstrous, Mr. Watson, beyond belief. My life has been dull but at least it has been safe from harm. Why couldn't my sister have been me? If I had been her, I swear I would have fought him and beaten him, even if I had to kill him! When I hear these things, I hate men and everything to do with them . . ."

Then seeming to realize that she was addressing someone who qualified for that category, she smiled timidly in apology and it was as though the sun had broken through for a moment. Now I could see the resemblance.

I also couldn't help remembering all those movies when the hero leans across, removed Miss Prim's glasses and lets her hair down before exclaiming—"Why, Miss Smith, you're *beautiful!*" I thought on balance that probably would not be a good tactical move on this occasion.

Then it was as if the fever had broken. She actually sat back a little in her chair. She tucked her tissue away somewhere and even crossed her legs. Her expression became thoughtful more than anguished.

"So why does she stay?" I asked to keep the conversational ball rolling. "Your sister is a grown woman. Is it the money?"

"Oh, no, she has put away plenty of money over the years and she could earn a lot more as a model or an actress, if she wanted to. My sister is a very beautiful woman . . ."

She raised her chin and said this last almost

defiantly, as if challenging me to disagree.

"Indeed, she is from what little I have seen of her. Indeed, you *both* are."

I said it in an attempt to be mock-gallant, then realized that I meant it. There was something about her that stirred the Sir Galahad in a lad.

She looked up momentarily from beneath her eyelids. "Yes, Miss Smith . . ." I thought.

Now she was all seriousness again. We were reaching the Big Finish.

"But the other day a terrible thing happened, which is why I am here today . . ."

She now took a delicate lace handkerchief from her purse and began to twist it between her fingers. As she did so, I caught the whiff of an expensive perfume that triggered a memory I could not quite catch. I nodded for her to continue.

"Mr. Kane had been particularly harsh to my sister. He treats her as if she were still a small child and she had done something to annoy him, which is not difficult to do. He had her locked in her room for three days as a punishment and forbade her to see her friends and one friend in particular—Nicky, who owns Birdland—the place I told you about

"When she was allowed out of her room, she was desperate to do something to spite him, so she stole something he values above all else and certainly above her . . ."

76

"The Borgia Bird," I said.

"Then you *know?* That *is* why he hired you? I knew it—we both knew it."

Then surprisingly she reached over and seized my hand in both of hers.

"Oh, Mr. Watson—may I call you Jack?—you must help us. If you find it—*when* you find it—I beg you to say nothing of her involvement. It would go very badly for her and I think already he suspects her. I'm sure you can find a way to prove to him she was not involved . . ."

I could feel a check for a thousand dollars burning a hole in my inside pocket. It focused the mind wonderfully.

"Why doesn't she simply put it back where she found it?" I have the kind of mind that cuts through the crap.

"Because she no longer has it. She—gave it away. I'm not sure but I think she got that vile Perlman person to help her."

"Gave it *away?*"

"She wanted no part of it. But she didn't want him to have it, either."

"Who did she give it to?"

Even as she said she didn't know, I knew she was lying through her pearly whites. It's little things like the way the thumb hovered near the mouth and the handkerchief got screwed up into a ball that tell us professionals what we need to know. Body language speaks louder than words.

And you may quote me: Watson's Wisdom.

I looked over to Holmes for confirmation but he was looking at the ceiling for some reason.

"Okay, then, so I'll have to talk to your sister." That snapped her out of it but fast.

"Oh, but you *mustn't!*"

"You mean, she's not been well and is easily upset?" I recalled the way Kane had explained things.

"Yes, but how did you know?"

"Tell her it is your business to know things that other people don't. That is your trade." It was Holmes's voice inside my head. So he hadn't been studying my peeling ceiling after all.

"It's my business to know things other people don't, honey," I heard myself say.

"That's my trade."

"And that's why you came here," Holmes added.

"And that's why you came here." Pretty impressive.

She seemed to think so. We had the eye routine again.

"I will—*we* will be guided by you, Jack, but could I ask that to begin with you let me be the go-between? Just until Nana grows more comfortable with the idea."

I nodded. There was little else a gentleman could do, particularly when a potential client is holding his hand as if both their lives depended on it.

"Since your father is my client, I can do nothing officially," I said gently, "but I'll see what I can do." That didn't come out quite as cogently as I'd intended. I prized her fingers off as considerately as I could.

She gathered her things together and got up to go.

"Nana and I will find some way to reward you, you have my word on it." And for the first time she looked me full in the eyes. Once again I caught a whiff of that elusive perfume. Who was the mousey sister now?

"How can I contact you?"

"Don't worry, Jack. I shall contact *you* . . ."

And with a walk that suggested for the first time that there was a woman under the dull gray dress, she left the office.

Following Holmes's earlier advice, I hurried to the window to watch Anna Kane cross the street. There was no doubt about it, I had clearly managed to give the lady newfound confidence. There was a lilt in her step. She was a different woman.

I turned back to my partners in crime.

"Well, Holmes? I thought I handled that pretty well."

"As I have often had occasion to tell you, Watson, the fair sex is your department and always has been. I bow to your abilities. The lady was clearly impressed by your grasp of the situation."

"What points struck you in particular, Holmes?" A little low animal cunning here. Pick *his* brains first.

"Oh, very much the ones that struck you, I imagine, old fellow. The curious case of the dog in the daytime, for instance . . ."

"The *dog?*"

"Yes, don't tell me you have forgotten the case of Silver Blaze, the champion race horse that was stolen. Surely you remember that the clue to the whole affair was the fact that the guard dog did *nothing* in the nighttime. It did not bark at the murderer, because it *knew* him."

"Ah—yes . . ."

"Similarly, Mike here—who normally takes an unhealthy interest in anyone new—stayed well away from Miss—Kane. Something about her disturbed him." He puffed thoughtfully on his pipe. I noticed that he had politely refrained from lighting it in Anna Kane's presence, even though it gave off no smell.

Then I had the answer. Obvious.

"It was probably her perfume. A little cloying. I noticed it myself."

"As, indeed, did I—even in my present 'state.' A woman's perfume is her signature, Watson, never forget it. I once identified seventy-five different perfumes—I even wrote a small mono-graph on the subject. By now I am sure there are many more but each of them is as individual as a fingerprint.

"The lady's sister was wearing the identical perfume this morning. It reached even me on the bend of the stairs as we entered the hall."

Of course. Holmes was right. That was where . . .

"Rich sister gives favorite perfume to poor sister to celebrate their renewed relationship. Women are always sharing personal things like that," I added knowledgeably.

"Possibly, Watson, possibly. They certainly have many tastes in common. Even though the day is hot and the other young ladies in the street outside are going about in the lightest of clothing that would have shocked Her Majesty considerably, you will have observed that both of *our* young ladies prefer to wear dresses with long sleeves. And, of course, you observed that all of Miss Anna's clothes were brand news?"

"How can you possibly be sure of that? She is clearly a careful woman?"

"Not careful enough to remove the price tag from the back of her dress. And did you not notice that she did not know where to find the pocket? A whole life may be determined by the wear on a sleeve or the hem of a dress. My first glance is always at a woman's sleeve. In a man it is perhaps better first to take the knee of the trouser.

"She also dropped something when she retrieved her handkerchief. You will find it just under your desk there."

I bent over and disinterred a crisp new business card from among the dust balls—

Anna K. Adam

"Adam," Holmes mused. "The primal name. Taken from her foster parents, I wonder? Or chosen to re-christen herself?"

But another thought was going through my mind that I didn't think worth bothering Holmes with at this point. By the way the type was set the initial letters stood in relief. Another way of looking at "Anna K. (K for Kane, despite her protestations?) Adam" was—

A.K.A.

Also Known As . . .

"Interesting, most interesting."

Abruptly Holmes put his pipe in his pocket. Presumably an imaginary pipe can't burn a hole in an imaginary suit?

"Oh, and there was one other thing I noticed . . ."

"Yes?"

"Far be it from me to interfere with your

present incarnation but really, Watson—'Chick!' *'Honey!'* You were brought up to speak the language of Shakespeare, Keats, Macaulay, Trollope. 'Oh, what a falling off was there . . .' *Hamlet*," he added.

"And now, old fellow, I suggest we resume our quest for antiques. Like us, none of them are getting any younger . . ."

And he gave that convulsive silent laugh that signified he had made and was enjoying a joke.

FIVE

I left with the feeling that my office had somehow turned into the concourse at Grand Central at rush hour. What had happened to that haven of peace, where on an average day—and there were plenty of *them*—I could sit and bet against myself as to which raindrop would reach the bottom of the windowpane first? And then cheat if I lost.

Where I could sit and commune for hours with my framed photograph of Raymond Chandler and crack wise back and forth out of the side of our mouths? *"Ou sont les longeurs d'antan?"* as he might have said—had he spent more time reading Georges Simenon. What I liked about the picture of Ray was that his expression said that he knew that I knew that he knew. And, frankly, I could do with a bit of that in my life.

The lobby was a Chinese-free zone. The only clue to their having paid us a visit the fact that Troy was sporting a paper cap that looked suspiciously like the one the phoney delivery boy had been wearing and a white jacket folded on top of Mrs. Plack's pile of "things."

"Finders keepers, Mr. Watson," she trilled merrily, when she saw me eyeing it. "It will do for my cousin's youngest boy." Having met her cousin's youngest, I made a mental note to avoid any Chinese restaurant he decided to work in. The boy didn't know his *dim sum* from his *bok choy*.

Troy & Plack—now *that's* not a bad name for an agency—had just given new meaning to "Chinese takeaway."

Quentin Mallory was the Thin Man. Not the Fat Man. Not the Tin Man. The Thin Man.

He was all of seven feet tall and it was as if that Baby Giant had been at play again, only this time, instead of squashing his play dough, he'd decided to stretch it as far as it would go without snapping. This was the result. If he'd been any taller, Quentin Mallory would have needed oxygen to breathe up in that rarified atmosphere.

So when I say that he looked down his nose at me when I introduced myself, I'm not making a value judgment—though he probably was. He struck me as being someone who didn't suffer fools gladly and I suspected his definition was catholic with a small "c."

He was black silk Armani from head to pointed Gucci toe and Georgio must have stood on an assistant's shoulders for the final fitting. Head was immaculately tousled silver and from the way he was constantly touching it and smoothing it, I guessed a rug. The second time I saw him I knew for sure.

It didn't even take all of my detecting skills to

make the politically incorrect assumption that the guy was of an alternative sexual persuasion. Jesus, I can still remember when "gay" meant cheerful and "fruit" was something you ate. But that way madness lies . . .

Mallory was certainly gay in both senses of the word. Now what could he do for me? A little bird—a sweet little *white* bird—had told him he might expect a visit from a *gorgeous* private detective. He held out a pale white hand. I shook it, projecting as much testosterone as I knew how.

"Goodness, what *have* I done, Mr. Watson? Have I been a bad boy? Oh, I do hope so! Will it be handcuffs and leg irons? As long as they don't leave a mark on my Armani. Take me—I'm yours!"

And with that he threw up his hands in mock horror until they disappeared in low lying cloud. The eyes—pale poached eggs in a face that would otherwise have graced a Roman coin—turned heavenwards. Which was nearer for him than most of us.

"Are you doing your stupid bitch act again?"

It came from somewhere much nearer the ground. I looked around and then down to find a stature-challenged person, who now began to tug at Mallory's trouser leg to get his attention. He must have been about three feet tall and seemed to have that concentrated aggression that I'm sure can easily come with being so—concentrated.

While he was tugging, he turned a baleful eye on me.

"Don't even *think* it," he said. "Don't think 'midget,' 'dwarf,' 'little person.' Think 'compact'—like in automobile. Think 'condensed'—as in milk. Think 'efficient performance.' "

Mallory had now rejoined us. Having detached the new arrival from his trouser leg, he was anxiously smoothing out the creases.

"I *hate* it when you do that. I know this is supposed to be 'unstructured' but there *are* limits, you little—*thing,* you. And I do object to 'bitch.' If you must use a female appellation, you may refer to me as 'Caesar's wife' who, as you know, was above reproach. Or in my case, perhaps *beneath* it!" He giggled girlishly. "Oh, yes, I think I'm safe in saying that, when it comes to gossip and secrets, I'm *definitely* beneath anything you care to name. Oh, dear, sometimes I'm so sharp I could cut myself."

Then, turning to me, he flashed a smile his orthodontist would have been proud of.

"I see you've met my assistant, Petit. A royal pain in just about any part of the anatomy but a genius when it comes to shaping metal. I managed to wean him away from Snow White, didn't I? Heigh-ho, heigh-ho. No, but seriously, I rescued this poor little mite from the Hollywood scrap heap. He'd come here hoping they were about to remake *The Wizard of Oz,* and he wanted to be the Head Munchkin, didn't you, sweet thing?"

And with that he scooped up the—compact person and deposited him on top of a glass showcase, where his little feet dangled dangerously above the ground.

"Big giraffe!" screamed the little man.

"Toadstool!" Mallory screamed back at him. "No—toad's tool!"

"Pencil dick!"

"Runt features!"

"Sperm crap!"

"No such word!" Mallory exclaimed triumphantly. This was obviously their little domestic routine trotted out to entertain first time visitors—and I had no intention of interrupting its natural course, being a great believer in the sanctity of hearth and home—always assuming one had either.

Petit looked pensive for a moment, then summoned up his best shot—

"But if there *were,* you'd be it!"

That seemed to satisfy both of them and Mallory lifted him gently down and ruffled his spiky hair, which is more that I'd have dared to do, since it had the approximate appearance of a porcupine. Mallory had certainly missed out on that one.

While the boys had been entertaining each other, I'd been glancing around the showroom and I could see that Holmes had been doing the same. Mike, on the other hand, was totally fascinated by the sight of its owner's bean pole legs. To him they must have seemed like the ultimate living lamp posts. His main dilemma was whether to christen them or to hump them. Fortunately, the indecision prevented him from doing either.

The place was an Aladdin's cave. It was as though Louis XIV had left him the entire contents of Versailles and then Chairman Mao had come along and said—"Look here, Quent, old man, we're going a bit minimalist here in China, so would you mind taking all this Chinoiserie crap off my hands?"

It was obvious where Kane's interior designer had shopped to furnish Kane Towers.

"Fun, isn't it? All those heavenly MGM movie sets crammed into one. You almost expect Garbo and dear John Gilbert to emerge from behind that chiffonier and as for that couch—isn't that pure Anna May Wong? Ah, what it is to be a snapper-up of well-considered trifles!

"I tell you, Mr. Watson—or may I call you Jack? I'm Quent to my friends and I feel we're friends already. Well, Jack, if you were to lift off the roofs of all the houses in Beverly Hills and Bel Air, you'd find them literally stuffed to the gills with Mallory antiques . . ."

"And most of them would be Mallory fakes." It was Holmes's voice in my ear, even though he was the other side of the showroom. While I was being subjected to the cabaret performance, he had been wandering about abstractedly, peering at details of the furniture with a magnifying glass. He had now mastered the disconcerting art of dematerializing and then reappearing somewhere else when least expected. It did not make for a comfortable coexistence.

"Mr. Kane has been one of our most regular customers. A gentleman of the most eclectic taste, Mr. Kane." There was that "eclectic" again. "But a little bird tells me you have come to discuss a little bird in the hand—or, as I hear, sadly no longer in the hand but in someone's bush. Oops, what have I said? Please follow me to Santa's workshop . . . Petit."

With that he gave the kind of bow and flourish totally appropriate to the court of the Sun King and ushered me through a door the little man was holding open.

The room we entered was a complete contrast. Stark and functional, it was set out with benches, tool racks and what looked like miniature furnaces. One whole side of the room was lined with shelves and cupboards from floor to ceiling. Propped against them was a tall rolling ladder, presumably to enable Petit to gain access to the higher levels.

Inside their private domain Mallory and Petit seemed to change, too. The outrageous behavior was set aside, as an actor sheds a role when he walks off stage. Petit hopped up on a counter and Mallory leaned against it like a tired stork, while I took the chair he indicated. Mike, his nose numbed by the cornucopia of varnish and paint smells, settled by my side. Holmes was doing his impersonation of the Invisible Man.

Mallory spoke in a businesslike tone.

"Mr. Kane has been a customer of ours for some years now. Since you are temporarily in his employ and he has sent you to me, I can be frank with you. He is living proof—at least for the time being—that money can't buy you taste. And even though that sentiment sounds reminiscent of an old Beatles song, it is an axiom I have seen proved time and again.

"Then one day he sent for me to that gothic monstrosity he calls home and there he showed me his pride and joy—the Borgia Bird. Could I—*would* I make him an exact copy, so that he could have his cake and masticate it in secret, so to speak? It is a *malaise* I have found to be quite common with the fanatical collector. The piece was complex but not impossible—not when you have a miniature Cellini, a foreshortened Fabergé at hand, all packed into the person of my small but perfectly-formed friend here."

I am no judge of how a diminutive person looks when he blushes but I would have laid a certain amount on the fact that Petit was blushing now. Even his "Ah, he's full of shit!" lacked true conviction. I realized that theirs was the surface badinage of an old married couple, a façade that kept the rest of the world at a distance. There was genuine affection between this oddest of odd couples. I rather envied them at that moment. After all, I had nobody at home to call me "sperm crap" except Mike and his vocabulary was a little limited.

"Fetch the Bird, if you would be so kind, *mon petit vieux . . .*"

Petit toddled over to one of the drawers and a moment later was back with two objects wrapped in velvet. His tiny fingers unwrapped the first with surprising delicacy and laid the contents on the countertop. There were the two halves of a mould into which metal would be poured.

He did the same with the second parcel and now, gleaming in the light from a table lamp, was the Borgia Bird—or, at least, a sibling facsimile of the one Kane had shown me this morning. Was it only this morning?

"Since I had gone to the trouble of hatching one for my client, I thought I would hatch another to keep it company on a need-to-know basis. And on this occasion I saw no reason why my client *needed* to know. He paid for what he got and now I have this pretty thing to keep me company on long winter evenings."

Mallory picked up the bird and stroked its feathers, as if they were real.

"I may not have the original but I have something else that Mr. Kane does not . . ."

"And that is?"

"Knowledge, Jack—knowledge. Kane believes what he wishes to believe about the Bird's provenance but *I* know—thanks to Petit here—that it is much older than he thinks. Show him, Petit."

The little man took the Bird from Mallory and brought it over to me, carrying it with the reverence a priest might show to communion wine.

"It's something you wouldn't notice by holding the creature as you would hold a real bird—in the palm of the hand. But when you are examining it all over, as I had to do to make sure the copy was perfect, I noticed this . . ."

He turned the Bird onto its back and with his stubby index finger indicated the area under the neck. To me they were a tangle of feathers but, as I looked more carefully, I thought I could discern certain hieroglyphics interwoven. I became aware of Holmes peering over my shoulder.

"Chinese characters, Jack, and very old ones at that," Mallory chimed in. "I have done a little discreet research and that particular script comes from a region in the north of China and dates back—wait for it—about three thousand years.

This little fellow was over two thousand years old before it became a toy for the Bloody Borgias. It is beyond price, my friend, beyond price."

That was the second time someone had told me that.

"And what does it say?"

"Ah, there we have unfinished business, I'm afraid. There are perhaps three scholars in the whole of the country who may be able to decipher the characters and they would certainly want to know why I wanted to know. Even to ask may give away the existence of the Bird and—who knows?—there may well be people out there with a genuine claim to it. And I am virtually certain that our friend, Osgood Kane—or whoever he really is—is not of their number. So there, for the moment, the matter must rest. Now, who was it who said that knowledge was power?"

Whoever it was I was not to learn, for at that very moment a bell indicated the presence of someone in the showroom outside. Well, I say "bell" but, in fact, it was another of those damn chimes. This time we were treated to "The hills are alive with the sound of music" played on a glockenspiel, which made me strangely nostalgic for "The Ride of the Valkyrie."

"Don't you just *love* Julie Andrews?" Mallory levered himself into an upright position and made for the door. "As Larry King likes to say—'Don't go away, now.' "

Petit busied himself rewrapping the birds and I was sitting contemplating what I had just been told, when I heard Mallory address whoever had arrived in the outer room . . . "Miss Kane, this is a pleasant surprise. Had I known you wished to see me, naturally I would have been happy to call upon you and save you this trouble . . ."

Miss Kane! I caught Holmes's eye and watched him shimmer towards the open door. To move myself would immediately alert Petit to my undue interest in the new arrival.

Now I could hear a woman's voice sounding tense and strained. Although I couldn't make out what she was saying, I recognized the tonality I had heard earlier in the entrance hall at Kane Towers.

Mallory was attempting to calm her.

"As you requested, I have attempted to intercede with the party in question. Without success, I'm afraid. He professes to be totally ignorant of the matter. It does not appear to be a question of money. There is something about the merchandise that seems to stick to the fingers of those who come into contact with it. If you will permit me to suggest it, your own special powers of persuasion might more easily prevail— always assuming he *is* the one in possession of the artifacts in question. As it happens, I have someone else making similar inquiries on behalf of your dear father. In fact, he is with me at this very moment . . ."

He must have indicated the inside room, for there were sounds of someone leaving in a hurry and the sound of music was once again heard in the land.

Mallory called out after her and did I detect a certain malice in his tone?

"Mr. Perlman will find the usual consignment in the trunk of his car . . ."

Moments later he was back.

"Such a sad situation, especially after all the trouble Petit and I took. As we have mutual interests in this matter, I feel I can confide in you, Jack. Miss Kane is, shall we say, 'romantically entangled' with one Nicky Parmentieri, the proprietor of a certain night club . . .

"Among others," he added after a moment's thought.

"Birdland," I added helpfully. It was about time I earned my detecting credentials.

"Oh, you know it?"

"Know *of* it."

"Well, it appears that on a whim—girls will be girls!—Miss Kane decided to transfer custody of the Bird from her father to someone else. To whom she refuses to say but an educated guess would suggest to Mr. Nick as a way of—shall we say?—cementing the relationship. Now she is exercising a lady's prerogative to change her mind but the putative new custodian is failing to reciprocate and, since he is also an excellent customer . . . You see my dilemma? . . . Show Jack Mr. Nick's toys, Petit."

Petit went over to another drawer and beckoned me over imperiously. We were on his turf now. He pulled it open and there lay row after row of ceramic birds. There were birds of paradise, parrots, bluebirds, doves, finches—and a whole row of miniature Borgia phoenixes.

"Birds, birds, birds. A symbolic bird like the phoenix I can understand but as for the rest . . ." The long thin nose wrinkled in exaggerated disgust. "Nasty, dirty creatures. Poe had it right. 'Nevermore,' quoth the Raven. My sentiments, precisely!"

"One would think Mr. Nick had quite enough without being so stubborn about one more but our little feathered friend—not you, Petit—has such winning ways. Nicky likes to give these to his favored customers and they make a nice little sideline for us, do they not, little one? Keeps my diminutive friend out of the saloons and bowling alleys. Which is as well—just in case someone decided to use him for a bowling ball."

He ruffled the little man's hair again and the patronizing gesture seemed to trigger his temper.

"And if *you* were on a croquet court, they'd use you as a mallet!"

"And *you* could be a bowling pin . . ."

"Stick insect!"

"Termite!"

I felt this was where I'd come in and I noticed that Holmes and Mike had already left.

"Well, goodbye, boys. I make it thirty-all." I said over my shoulder and heard Mallory interrupt his tirade long enough to call out—

"Follow the Yellow Brick Road, Jack . . . and remember—surface impressions can be deceptive."

As I joined my compadres in the street outside, I could still hear in the distance . . .

"What's the weather like up there?"

"Must be cold down in the primordial slime . . ."

Holmes was looking thoughtful. "Our friend Mallory hides a sharp mind behind that frivolous façade, though I fear it may prove double-edged, if he is not careful. He believes himself to be in possession of the facts and, indeed, he knows more than Kane—but still not enough."

"In what way, Holmes?"

"For example, he has deduced—quite rightly—that the so-called Borgia Bird is, in fact, Chinese in origin and very ancient Chinese at that. This may well explain the current interest of our Chinese visitors. What he has failed to decipher is the *meaning* of the inscription. I have, as you will doubtless remember, made some small study of Chinese dialects and characters. I am open to correction but I am prepared to assert that the letters on the breast of the phoenix read—

" 'MY KISS IS DEATH'

"Don't forget, the phoenix is a symbol of rebirth. But before rebirth comes death. The latter is a certainty. The former? Something of a gamble, I would have thought. Take my word, the Bird bodes no good to anyone who owns it, Watson."

"And right now his name is Nicky Parmentieri?"

"So it would appear. Oh, and one other thing, old fellow. Am I to infer that you have become a member of the Masons or some other secret order that insists on your wearing their insignia on the inside of your coat lapel?"

I fumbled under the collar of my jacket and found myself holding a small metal button-like object backed with velcro. I recognized it immediately for what it was.

"My God, Holmes," I exclaimed. "A bug!"

"Surely not, old fellow. It appears to be metallic in origin."

I explained as best I could the nature of the device and I saw his eyes light up.

"Ingenious, my dear Watson. What a boon such a thing would have been to us during our glory days." Then another thought struck him.

"But then, what would have happened to the excitement of making deductions from fragments of fact and inference, from piecing together the mosaic of behavior and event when one could simply have sat back in Baker Street and listened to a miscreant hang himself from his own lips? No, old friend, I would not exchange the theatre of the questing mind for all your modern technology."

As he spoke, my mind was racing back over the past few hours and then it came to me.

"Kai-Ling! Do you remember, Holmes, when we entered Kane's house he insisted on brushing my coat. I thought he was simply being orientally overattentive. When he smoothed down my jacket, that must have been when he placed the bug."

"So he and his friends have presumably heard every word you have said and every word said to you since we left Kane? Hm. But that does not explain one thing."

"Which is?" I asked, as I dropped the infernal device in a nearby trash bin. Let the Chinese interpret the mumbles and grunts of the first street person to rummage through it.

"How they could *see* what you were doing in your office.

"And incidentally, old fellow, I think we should be making tracks, if we are to keep our quarry in sight. When Miss Nana left in such a hurry, faithful friend Perlman was once again waiting for her with the Porsche. They had something of an altercation, he checked the boot—I believe you call it the 'trunk' for some strange reason—and they are even now turning on to the highway over there."

A few moments later the Corvette was making the identical turn.

SIX

Dusk was falling as we headed back up into the hills. Inky fingers were beginning to infiltrate the sunshine like an unnatural blonde whose roots are starting to show. Ah, Marlowe, eat your heart out!

A clapped-out Corvette is no match for a Porsche but I wasn't worried. I knew where Nana Kane and Brent Perlman were going.

Sure enough, we made one more turn in the road and up ahead of us a huge neon bird was poised for flight.

This one was a Bird of Paradise—all plumes and attitude. You've never seen a bird more pleased with itself. It was sitting on the word BIRDLAND as if it fully expected to hatch it.

As I pulled into the parking lot, I could see the Porsche. It was parked askew in the Owner's slot, which was likely to piss him off a lot when he saw it. There was no sign of Nana Kane, though the passenger door was left pointedly open, as though she was in too much of a hurry to shut it.

White Suit—I still couldn't think of him as anything else—was unloading cardboard boxes from the trunk. If you can unload boxes morosely, then that's what he was doing.

I parked the Corvette in a remote corner of the

lot. It was also memorable—though, alas, not for the same reason as the Porsche—and I didn't want to be remembered.

The neon bird now began to show off outrageously. A myriad little lights in its "feathers" began to wink on and off and its beak to open and close. I saw Holmes's mouth open in emulation before he realized what he was doing and turned in my direction. His "Oh, Watson! That it should come to this!" did not strike me as being unqualified approval.

I found that more and more I was beginning to see my world through his eyes and, frankly, it took some explaining. Heigh-ho.

I turned my attention to Mike.

"This place isn't fit for man or dog, old buddy, so we're going to have to divide our forces." I find it always helps to explain one's reasoning. "I'll take on the dangers of the cocktail bar and you guard the jalopy. *Guard!* OK? I may be some time."

The word "Guard" always makes his ears prick up and his teeth unsheath, ready to be sunk into the nearest enemy object. I've saved a fortune on car alarms since I met Mike. And now that I've trained him to understand that he doesn't have to guard against *me,* we're doing fine.

Holmes and I sauntered up to the doors of the gilded bird cage as to the manner born.

"Watson, let us divide our forces, too. I suggest

that I—in your curious new parlance—'case the joint,' while you take up a strategic position so that you can see who comes and goes."

Right. Starsky & Hutch, Cagney & Lacey, Watson & Holmes. Correction—Holmes & Watson.

Inside the club, to be fair, a certain degree of taste did prevail. There was a deal of red plush and subdued lighting and the bird motif was restricted to a series of subtly-illuminated paintings by famous artists—Audubon, Henri Rousseau, Matisse and so on—that were clearly copies but good ones.

Holmes found it difficult to understand why one of them should be of a black gentleman holding a saxophone called Charlie Parker and captioned "Bird" but we surmounted that hurdle and moved on. In fact, before I knew it Holmes had vanished entirely.

There were tables and banquettes in a loose semicircle around a small stage at one end of the room. On it a group of chorines dressed in—you've guessed it—feathers—were prancing around, while one of their number, dressed as a baby chick, sang something on the lines of—

Come on, honey, muss my feathers,
Come on, honey, peck my cheek—
Doesn't matter what the weather's,
I'm the chick to tweak your beak . . .

Should any of the more inebriated customers have felt inclined to take her up on her offer, there were several gorilla-related gentlemen posted around the periphery of the room to persuade them otherwise.

The whole of the left-hand side of the room was taken up with a long bar behind which a mirror reflected the rest of the room. I decided that this was my strategic command post and took a seat there.

Chickie gave up her plea for companionship and the girls took over in a sort of avian can-can, at the end of which they threw cotton-wool eggs into the audience and exited to scattered applause.

It was only in the comparative silence that ensued that I realized there was a competing entertainment at the far end of the room.

An ornately-decorated set of wooden doors gave on to what was presumably an office. Suddenly they were wrenched open and Nana Kane stormed out. On the threshold she paused and turned to address someone in the room behind her.

It was the first clear view of the woman that I had had and I can vouch for the fact that an angry woman can be beautiful. There was a flush on the patrician cheekbones and the shoulder-length black hair was charmingly disheveled—or at least not noticeably sheveled. But then she could have been dragged through a hedge backwards, forwards and sideways and still have been worth looking at. At the same time the eyes projected the heat of several microwaves working in sync.

I would not have cared to be on the receiving end of what she was microwaves saying—the most remarkably articulate set of obscenities and epithets I think I have ever heard and these shell-like ears have been affronted more often than I care to recall. I wish I'd made notes. They would have come in handy in years to come.

She finished by recommending to her target that he commit a sexual act of impossible proportions and then blazed a trail to the front door, passing me en route.

The likeness to her sister Anna was remarkable, uncanny . . . two peas in a pod doesn't begin to describe it. And yet . . . these were two distinct personas—*personae*? Who cares? Like positive and negative film images. The one distinct, the other a blurred shadow.

I felt a sudden twinge in a part of my metabolism I'd thought long since calcified. When the light caught her a certain way Nana Kane reminded me of a lovely lady I was once briefly married to. But that was in another country and, besides, the wench is dead.

As she passed me, she looked at me fleetingly and what was that expression I read in her eyes? Despair? A child's fear?

Then the door banged shut behind her and the familiar sound of a Porsche shredding its tires was the next sound to be heard.

I contemplated following her but instinct told me that what I needed to know next was here in this room. I turned back to the bar and exchanged looks with the bartender. It's remarkable how two sets of eyebrow movements can convey—

"That's women for ya!"

and—

"What can ya do?"

He read me like a used book and brought me a Jack Daniel's on the rocks.

We private eyes have to be proficient in Mirror Work 101. This involves sitting in bars and surveying the room in the mirror opposite, always remembering that what you're seeing is backwards. This is grueling work and gets harder the more Jack D. insists on keeping Jack W. company.

But the face that appeared over my shoulder was no hardship at all backwards or forwards.

Long auburn hair in a Veronica Lake peek-a-boo page-boy bob, a touch of the sultry Yvonne de Carlo about the full scarlet mouth and eyes that looked up from lowered lids that were meant to make you recall the way Bacall looked at Bogie in *To Have and Have Not*. And if you are too young to pick up the references—tough.

"You look like the kind of guy a girl could bum a cigarette from."

Now, what can you say to that? They don't write lines like that anymore. I fumbled my pack of Camels out of my pocket. I rarely smoke but you have to be ready for moments like this.

She leaned over me and I caught a blast of something exotic rising to meet me. *Fleurs du mal*, I shouldn't wonder. She took two cigarettes and put both of them between lips the color of a rogue fire engine.

"Match me!"

And then it all fell into place.

She was doing the Paul Henreid/Bette Davis schtick from *Now, Voyager*. Warner Brothers 1942—except with the roles reversed, as befits an age of enlightened feminism. Bette Davis reconstructed in *Forever Tomorrow*, a 1978 TV movie starring . . . Linda Grace.

And here was I being fed a lipstick-stained cigarette by a legend of the silver screen. Should I ask her to autograph my coaster? Or would a simple grovel on one knee suffice?

Linda Grace distracted me at this point by leaning over still further to reach the ash tray on the bar, revealing a cleavage that was generous to the point of being spendthrift. The ignoble sexist thought—"You don't get many of those to the kilo"—raced through my pubescent brain and, luckily, out the other side. I vowed to say an infinite number of Hail Marys to Mrs. Pankhurst at some future date.

I wrenched my mind back to listen to what the goddess was saying.

"I must apologize for that little scene back there, Mr.—?"

"Watson. Jack Watson."

"I'm afraid my stepdaughter is a rather troubled person at present but that is no excuse for interrupting the social life of others. She is a young lady of strong, if misguided, convictions. Personally, I like my convictions diluted—same as I do my bourbon."

I can take a hint. I used the dumb show hand signals drinkers and bartenders recognize the world over.

"I have a confession to make." She leaned even closer—no mean feat. Was it Groucho Marx or Bob Hope who said—"If I stood any closer, I'd be behind you"?

"That isn't *my* line. Bette Davis said it in *Jezebel*. I use it all the time. Never fails."

And to underline that she was joking, she nudged me playfully with something warm, soft and considerable. "By the way, my name is Linda—Linda Grace Kane."

"I don't care about your name. Keep the name! It's your soul I want . . ." I heard myself say.

The sculpted chin dropped. A little "work" there but let's not be picky. For a lady who must be well into her fifties she looked amazing. A few fine lines around the eyes but, hey, all the best people have laughter lines. Mine are practically hysterical.

Then she "got" it.

"My God, *Devil Queen*! My first starring role. Opposite dear old Seymour Blunt. An absolute darling but his sibilants gave him hell. So you know who I am? Or was? Just as I've just realized who you are. I thought the name rang a bell. You're going to get Osgood's bloody bird back for him . . ."

She offered me a porcelain hand to shake and, after a little juggling with cigarettes and shot glasses, I managed to do so. Her grip was firm and lasted rather longer than it strictly needed to and the eye contact that went with it was practiced and unblinking.

"It isn't too often that I meet a dyed-in-the-wool fan these days, Mr. Watson. Oh, I can't call you Mr. Watson, not when you're practically family, can I—Jack?"

And she raised the glass she'd been nursing in a toast to the mirror. From the color of it the bartender knew when not to say "when."

"You know, you private eyes—what do you call yourselves? Peepers? Gumshoes? Yuck, sounds like you stepped in something!—you interest me strangely."

And the lady was beginning to interest me

rather more predictably, for I could again feel the pressure of something soft and distinctly female against my arm. As far as I could tell it was warm and contained no bones. It might have been a cantaloupe she was taking home for later—but somehow I doubted it.

"Jack—I don't normally tell this to people but I'm quite physic—I mean psychic . . ."—the Jack D. was beginning to kick in—"and I think you are going to be my lucky mascot. 'Cos you know about Cinema. Not plain old movies—but *Cinema* . . ." She tried to mime quotation marks with the hand that held the glass. Enough of it slopped over me so that I wouldn't be thirsty for days. I could just lick my wrist.

"Tomorrow's a big day for me, Jack. B.I.G. Day! You want to know why?"

Any gentleman would want to know why. "Why?"

"Going back to work. Haven't worked since I married Mr. K. but the studio called and what's a girl to do? Had to be Linda Grace. I said, 'What about Glenn Close? Get Meryl Streep.' They said, 'No, got to have Linda Grace to play Linda Grace.' Well, that figures. Right?"

"Right."

"Want you to come along, Jack. Lucky mascot. Superior Studios. Little indie outfit over in Santa Monica. Tomorrow. Promise?"

One more move on her part and we'd be sharing

the same bar stool. I knew when I was beaten. Anyway, it would be a good learning experience for Holmes and Mike. You never knew, they might need a slightly-trained dog.

"Promise."

"Now then, Linda, you really mustn't bully Mr. Watson. From what I hear he has his hands full bird-watching. I doubt that he has time to go star-watching, too. Good evening, Mr. Watson and welcome to Birdland, my little fantasy world. May I introduce myself—Nicky Parmentieri. In simple language, I own the joint."

I found myself looking at the reflection of a young man of about thirty. He cut a slim figure and his tailor had cut the cloth of his expensive suit accordingly. The face was handsome to the point of being almost pretty but without looking in any way effeminate.

The hair was dark, almost black, and shiny. He had it brushed flat to his head and I wondered if this was a conscious imitation of the late George Raft.

It was the eyes that gave him away. Black and dead. This was a man who could "do" charm but didn't *feel* charm. Knowing a little of his background, I put him down as one of those who can smile and smile and be a villain. Such men, I knew from experience, are dangerous.

"Heard a lot about you, too, Nick," I said, as we matched macho handshakes. A draw.

"You having any luck finding Kane's Bird? That ditzy daughter of his seems to think *I've* got it for some reason and won't take no for an answer. One more scene like this evening and she's barred from here. She can take her elegant ass somewhere else. She's a classy lady but who needs the hassle?"

Methinks the gentleman doth protest too much.

"A few leads, yeah. We're getting there," I lied. The royal "We."

"Glad to hear it, 'cause I'd really like to make this thing go away. If there's anything I can do, short of dealing with Miss Trouble, you let Nicky know, you hear? I got plenty of friends I can call on . . ."

I just bet you have, I thought, and I bet most of their names sound like a form of pasta.

He turned his attention to Linda, who was now checking her makeup in the mirror and having trouble seeing over the row of bottles. Time for beddy-byes, Miss Grace . . .

Nick obviously shared my estimate of the situation.

"Hey, c'mon, Miss Movie Star," he said, taking her by the elbow, "you've got to look that camera in the eye first thing tomorrow, so you'd better be bright-eyed and bushy-tailed. Time you hit the road to Dream Land . . ."

Or Clichéville.

But before he got a reaction from La Grace, I

spotted Holmes hovering at my shoulder and indicating the door. Perlman had just entered looking distinctly uncomfortable.

Without taking in my presence—my back was, after all, turned to him—he approached Nick and began talking to him in an audible whisper.

"Jesus Christ, Nicky, the most terrible thing just happened. I'd unloaded the stuff and that mad woman rushed out and backed the damn car over the lot. It's ruined but I couldn't help it, Nicky!"

"Mr. Parmentieri to you, Perlman, and I'm sure Mr. Watson doesn't want to be bored by our domestic affairs. I suggest you wait in my office."

White Suit—once again a little grubby round the edges—couldn't wait. He scooted off like the White Rabbit in heat. Oh, my fur and whiskers!

Nicky pointed a smile my way that lacked any real conviction and I helped him hoist Linda into an ambulant posture. As he walked her towards his office, she sketched a queenly wave over her shoulder.

"*Ciao. Domani.*"

To which Nick added—

"Any time, Jack. Any time."

Then to Linda—

"Come on, duchess—time to powder your nose."

Holmes and I were alone with our mirror images.

"Well, Holmes, did you 'case the joint'?" It did, indeed, sound a strange phrase.

"Undoubtedly Mr. Parmentieri intended a play on words there but he touches upon the essence. This place is a powder keg in every sense. On the surface, Watson, this is a somewhat gaudy tinsel tavern, no better and no worse than its Victorian equivalents that housed the riff-raff of London. But for some of his wealthier and *louche* customers it is an exchange and mart for any drug they can afford to purchase.

"Oh, there is nothing overt about it, old fellow," he added, seeing my questioning expression. "The transaction is conducted in the simplest possible way. As I made my peregrinations around the room, I was able to see everything that transpired. If only I had been able to sit at the elbow of my suspects in the past, how much easier it would have been to bring those felons to justice! However . . .

"Certain patrons—presumably those previously cleared by the management—would order from the menu and ask for 'Today's Special.' The waiter would then ask them—'What number Special?' According to their answer, they were specifying the nature of the drug they required. He would then ask whether they required a 'starter portion' or an '*entrée* portion.' They would then be served a perfectly normal meal but, when they had paid the bill and were leaving, they would be handed—along with their receipt—one of friend Mallory's ceramic birds, 'as a token gift from the management.' From what I could determine— and I may be inaccurate in some of the detail—a dove contains marijuana, a blue bird something they referred to as 'LSD'—which in my day was a term that referred to currency but so be it. The bird of paradise was cocaine . . ."

"And the phoenix?"

"Heroin, without a doubt. The harbinger of death. Or should I say—'the *kiss* of death'? Perlman was the conduit for both the contents and the containers. I find it difficult to believe he did not know what they were used to contain. Hence the little difference of opinion we just witnessed.

"And you, Watson—what have *you* discovered?"

"Only that our friend Nick enjoys *both* the ladies of the Kane household. He and Linda are clearly what we would call an 'item' and I suspect that Nana Kane is now well aware of the fact that Nicky's affections are, shall we say, diluted and that he has his hands on *both* birds. Furthermore, my knowledge of the fair sex—which you seem determined to overstate—tells me that someone as tightly strung as Nana is not likely to take that well. A storm warning is imminent."

Holmes nodded thoughtfully.

"And what is more I do believe we have worn out our welcome in this hostelry, old fellow. I gained the distinct impression that Master Nick did not take kindly to what he perceived as your trespassing on his domain. I would be inclined to recommend a dignified retreat, followed by a short detour to the Cheeky Chicken to placate Mike . . . and then as good a night's sleep as we can contrive. Tomorrow, I fancy will not be without incident."

SEVEN

That night I slept like a log—though why a log sleeps any more soundly than a brick or a bag of plumber's tools beats me.

Somewhere along the way I began to dream. I was standing outside the Pearly Gates and banging on them for dear life. Though, come to think of it, if I was at that particular location, I was most probably dead.

Try as I might, I couldn't get anyone to open up. St. Peter was probably on his cell phone giving the Big Boss an update on yesterday's intake and the rest were watching daytime soaps, for all I knew.

Then I realized that the knocking was coming from the other side of the gate. St. Peter wanted to be let *out*.

Eventually it penetrated my befuddled brain that the knocking was at my front door and, if it hadn't had the desired effect on me, it was driving Mike apeshit. I clawed my way to the surface of sleep and staggered over to the door.

Standing there was a sandy little man in a suit that was so creased it made my pajamas look like permapress. Screwed into his mouth was the chewed butt of an unlit cigar.

"I thought a Private Eye was ever open?"

"Christ, McNulty—what do *you* want this time of the morning?"

"No, not Christ, Jack. Simple *Lieutenant* McNulty will do fine. And this time of the morning is damn near noon."

He pushed me gently but firmly aside, came into the room and looked around him. I thought the slight curl of the mouth at its somewhat bohemian appearance was good coming from a man in a suit like that.

Mike rushed up to him and pranced about on his hind legs like one of the chorus girls at Birdland. The dog was shameless.

"I could run you in for starving a great dog like this. Lucky for both of you I brought some emergency supplies." And from a baggy jacket pocket he pulled a handful of dog biscuits that had somehow got themselves entangled with his handcuffs. Mike whisked them off McNulty's palm like a croupier removing your losing chips and retreated to the settee.

The sight of the cuffs seemed to remind McNulty that this was more than his usual social visit. With a sigh he sank into the good chair, quite unaware that he was sitting on top of Holmes, who reappeared—looking a little ruffled, I thought—in the only other chair. Which left me standing.

Sean McNulty and I go back a long way—right back to the time when we were both sergeants in the L.A.P.D. Two of L.A.'s finest we were back then but somehow the routine and the toeing of lines wasn't for me and a couple of cases that had to be solved a certain way for "political reasons" did it and I quit. By now I'd be like McNulty, streetwise, world weary and with a wary eye peeled for the pension—as long as some punk kid with a homemade pistol and a head full of fantasy dust didn't decide to pop me one some night in a dark alley. Sure, that could happen in my business, too, but *I'd* be the one who made the decision to walk down that mean street.

In my line of business sometimes you walked— mostly you didn't. But the great thing about being self-employed is that you can be self-*un*employed without the accompanying social stigma.

Our ways had parted but McNulty and I—in all these years I'd never learned to call him Sean and I was still "Watson" to him—we kept in touch on an occasional basis. He was divorced and I was a widower, so what the hell. When the dark clouds overwhelmed the silver linings for either of us, we'd find the lowest dive in the neighborhood and get shit-faced. We'd show them.

But somehow I didn't think this was a social call.

"You know Brent Perlman."

It was a statement not a question.

"Guy in the white suit. Sure. Works for my client, Osgood Kane." Where was this going?

121

"*Worked.* Washed up on the shore at Santa Monica in the early hours. A floater.

"When did you see him last?"

No client confidentiality problem here that I could see, so I told him about our various sightings, ending with the incident at Birdland.

McNulty got up and started to pace the small room—no mean feat—rubbing his hand on his thinning pate. When you get to be a lieutenant you have to be able to do two things at once.

"That checks." Then he turned and peered at me. "Shouldn't tell you this and I'll deny it under oath—see, my fingers are crossed—but we've had you followed ever since you took Kane's shilling. No, don't worry, it's not Kane we're after.

"For once we don't give a shit about Kane. It's Perlman we've had our eye on.

"He's got another scam going with Nicky Parmentieri. Drugs. Big time. And we think our friend in the white suit has been the middle man for bringing in the happy dust and whatever else Nick is pushing."

A thought seemed to strike him and he sketched a smile.

"You know a funny thing? Word on the street is that old man Kane used to have this turf and Nicky has edged him out. And that's not the only thing of the old man's he's got his hands on."

"You mean the daughter?"

"Right. And through her he's got the run of the Kane place. You could park Concorde in the garage and the old man'd never know. The girl's probably in on it and Perlman keeps her quiet with a few free samples . . ."

Yes, indeed, that would account for a lot.

". . . takes it over to Chez Nicky, who dispenses it to the happy campers. Everybody comes out ahead. Except those who get a little too happy with it and end up dead. And talking of happy . . . call us chintzy but we don't like it on our patch. Well, it looks like the bag carrier just dropped the bag on his foot—or rather, somebody dropped it for him. Any ideas?"

He sank back into the chair.

"Well, Perlman wasn't exactly top of Nicky's hit parade at the last count . . ."

"Yeah, I guess 'hit' just about sums it up. See, something else you need to know about young Nicky. Birdland didn't just turn up in a Christmas cracker. It ain't even Nicky's at all. He was put in to manage it by the Pomona Family from St. Louis. Kind of a marker on Californian turf for them. The kid's a kind of son to the old man, Alfredo Pomona. Some people will tell you he is a son. Sort of freelance effort, if you know what I mean. Nicky makes it here and he's a made man—on the fast track. He can't afford to fuck up. You don't make it with one of the families and you're not only just a *made* man—you're a dead one wearing concrete Guccis. Even if you are sort of family.

"Best guess is Nicky had one of his guys bump off Perlman. There's a single bullet hole in the back of the neck—execution style. Then they'd take him in one of their delivery vans—which has now been hoovered to a fare-thee-well, you may depend—and dumped him. There's just one thing that doesn't fit the pattern . . ."

"What's that?"

"It's a business to these guys. They don't screw around. Bump. Dump. Thank you and goodnight. Why would they cut his finger off?

"His finger. *The* finger." And he demonstrated with a graphic gesture which finger he meant. "Nothing personal." A wry thought struck him. "Yeah, they gave him the ultimate finger. Funny, no—in a sick sort of way?"

McNulty levered himself to his feet, sighed, and made a desultory effort to smooth the creases out of his suit.

"Let me know if you find anything, Watson. And don't forget—the eyes of L.A.'s finest never sleep! We'll get that little squirrel Parmentieri. You have the word of the Pride of the McNultys."

The door slammed behind him and Mike gave a small yip of farewell.

"Your friend reminds me of no one as much as our old friend, Lestrade, Watson. Small, ferret-like but no doubt tenacious as a bulldog, when pointed in the right direction."

Holmes had returned to his original chair.

"Something about the mouth, too, the closeness of the eyes—and, of course, the mangled syntax."

He tapped his long fingers together thoughtfully.

"So drugs are one thread that runs through this tangled skein. Perlman was supplying Nana Kane to buy her silence and cooperation. I suspect it was becoming a moot point as to who was in charge of whom. And then Perlman over-played his hand . . ."

"You mean he had too much on Nicky?"

"Precisely, old fellow. If by that you mean incriminating information. *He* was now the weak link and people like Mr. Parmentieri—with his, shall we say, strict upbringing—do not like to be so beholden to a mere supplier. Friend Perlman was becoming potentially dangerous. His concern now must be to secure an alternative source of supply."

"But the severed finger?"

"That, I confess, is a piece of the puzzle that presently does not fit. Perhaps more will be revealed to us at your place of business . . ."

I don't know how chlorine combines with smog but the two seemed to be doing battle over The Century Building as we arrived. Mike and Mrs. Plack went through their usual routine but it lacked its usual "edge," for the good lady seemed a mite preoccupied. Having polished the lobby, she seemed to be contemplating tackling the sidewalk outside. I've heard of "house-proud" but "sidewalk-proud"?

The sight of me snapped her out of it.

"I had no idea you were such a Chinese food fan, Mr. W.," she shrieked, the twin "fs" giving her dentures a little trouble. "I told him you weren't in yet but he insisted on leaving it outside your door. Wasn't wearing one of those little white coats today," she added wistfully, "I suppose they only leave those with first time customers."

She was wasting her time with the last part. Holmes, Mike and I were ankling our way up the stairs.

Mrs. P. was incorrect in only one regard. The delivery boy had decided on door-to-desk delivery and he had achieved it by kicking the door in. Admittedly, it was a feat that could have been achieved by the most lissome member of the *corps de ballet* while executing his *entrechat*, but even so it meant more work for Troy.

There in the middle of my desk was the by now familiar brown paper bag. The three of us stared at it intently—two of us for professional reasons, the other out of sheer greed. I opened it and tipped out the contents—a waxed cardboard box and the inevitable fortune cookie.

First the box. Nestling in a bed of bamboo

126

shoots was a single spring roll. Before I could stop him, Mike had turned his head sideways and scooped it up. Now he had it hanging out of his mouth but instead of chomping it in his usual vigorous fashion, he turned to me with a puzzled expression. I could see why he might. Chicken or shrimp he was used to in his spring rolls. A human finger he was not.

Protruding from the end of the roll—rather as though the dog was putting his tongue out at me—was the tip of a male finger.

I have to admit it was an elegant finger, the nail neatly trimmed with a clear polish. The last time I had seen it was making up a set of five at the end of an arm in a white suit.

"It might be of minor interest to see what the accompanying message has to say, Watson."

Pausing only to retrieve the rest of Brent Perlman from Mike who, for some strange reason, seemed to have temporarily lost his appetite, I cracked the cookie and extracted the rice paper . . .

"HE WHO TOUCHES THE FORBIDDEN
LOSES THE POWER TO TOUCH"
—Confucius (trans.)

I picked up the phone and dialed a number I knew by heart. When he picked up, I said—

"McNulty. I seem to have something you were

missing. Afraid I don't do deliveries. You want to pick it up? Or shall I send it by FedEx?"

His answer almost melted the phone line. He'd pick it up and I wasn't to leave until he got there.

No sooner had I put the receiver down than it rang again.

"Good morning, Mr. Watson. We really must stop not meeting like this. But that, of course, is very much up to you.

"We are patient people, Mr. Watson. After all, we have waited many hundreds of years to reclaim what was ours to begin with but time, alas, is running out. The Bird's millennium is rapidly approaching and it must be returned to its ancestral home by that time for its symbolic rebirth, so you will appreciate our sense of urgency in this inconvenient matter.

"I should warn you and anyone else concerned that not only are we determined but we are— what is the word?—ubiquitous? Omnipresent? You will see Chinese faces everywhere you look and you will never know which are ours, for do we not all look alike to you? Just as you all look alike to us, by the way!

"Oh, and incidentally, I really must apologize for the so-called quotations from that rather boring man, Confucius. I have a colleague who is determined to find a saying to suit every eventuality and, frankly, he would do better to stick to Shakespeare or Oscar Wilde. I had to be extremely firm when he wanted to use something along the lines of—

"IF THY PRIVATE EYE OFFEND THEE—PLUCK IT OUT!"

I told him that a *mélange* of a 6th Century BC Chinese pseudo-sage, the Bible and Californian street *argot* was most definitely not something I cared to subscribe to.

"However, we all have our crosses to bear—as my old Oxford tutor was unduly fond of saying.

"Now, I can tell by the way you are prodding it around your desk that Mr. Perlman's inquisitive digit is concerning you. Just to set your mind at rest, Mr. Watson, we did not kill that rather incompetent meddler. No, that was a simple matter of thieves falling out. We did, however, *find* the somewhat soggy remains and took a little souvenir. Call it a marker. Next time we may be forced to leave our own mark first, which would be—as I am sure you will agree—*infra dig*. Do bear that in mind, my dear chap, won't you? Time is running out—but then, so are the usual suspects. I'd hate to think you were one of them. I was only saying to my colleagues here that you were looking particularly macho this morning. That—what do you call it?—'designer stubble' suits you, it really does. Ah well, I mustn't tie up your phone line any longer. We all have places to go, people to see. *A bientôt*, old chap."

The buzzing of electronic bees told me he had disconnected. I didn't need to relay the conversation to Holmes. Somehow he had the knack of tuning in when he wanted to.

"I wonder what wisdom Confucius has to offer us on the subject of *eyes,* old fellow?"

"What do you mean, Holmes?"

"The insect device enabled our Chinese friends to *hear* what was said but they are clearly able to both see and observe you—at least while you are in this room."

"Holmes, what a blind beetle I have been!" I expostulated. Now, to the best of my knowledge, I have never expostulated in my life and the only person I know who has ever used that phrase was floating next to me. What with his circumlocutions and an Oxford-educated Fu Manchu, I was rapidly getting out of my depth. On the other hand if I was honest, I hadn't felt so alive in years. I might have forgotten to shave in my hurry this morning, but that was a detail.

I decided to commune with my old pal Ray. Chandler's photo has stood me in good stead this many a year. The expression is sufficiently laconic that I can read into it whatever I choose. Amused resignation. Controlled irritation. Today, however, there was something different. I had never known him to wink at me. Yet there he was, one eye conspiratorially closed.

And then the dime dropped.

I unhooked the picture from the wall. Ray would wink all the way from here to eternity, for someone had cut the eye out of his picture. Behind him was a little electronic gizmo about the size of a playing card that had been using him as its own private eye. Raymond Chandler, Commie spy.

"Farewell, my lovely!" I expostulated (again), as I ripped the second infernal device from the wall and dumped it in the water cooler. Thus perish all villains!

"Hm," was all Holmes could contribute to the proceedings. "Who would have thought the Chinese would have attained such a degree of technical proficiency? In our earlier day, Watson, they were given to scurrying along darkened alleys with pigtails, large knives and incomprehensible imprecations. Remarkable.

"But this, I imagine, heralds the arrival of your friend McNulty?"

For the last several moments the sounds of police sirens had been fighting for supremacy with the varied background noises of a typical Los Angeles working day. Now with a sudden crescendo they stopped immediately below us and a few moments later an out of breath McNulty was among us, closely followed by an equally winded sergeant in uniform. McNulty has been here often enough to view the rapacious elevator as infinitely more of a health risk than the chance of cardiac arrest. His sergeant did not appear to have been given the option.

We all waited politely while McNulty gingerly prodded the disembodied digit with a pencil, before nodding to his assistant to commit it to an evidence bag, which he did even more gingerly.

"Looks like it, right enough. Want to tell me about it?"

Which I did. Mostly.

"Come in and make a statement later. OK? And keep in touch—specially if you get any more special deliveries."

At the door a thought struck him.

"I've heard of *lady* fingers—but that's Indian food, ain't it? Close but no cigar, huh? Here, pooch."

He indicated the remainder of the spring roll but Mike pretended he was licking his paw and hadn't heard.

We were alone again until, a moment later, McNulty's head appeared around the door and he flicked a folded piece of paper onto my desk.

"Somebody left this in your pigeonhole downstairs. Forgot to give it to you."

And he was gone again.

Well, at least it wasn't another fortune cookie and I deduced that it was a long shot Confucius had taken to writing notes, so it was probably safe to open it. But before I could do so, Holmes spoke—

"Come, Watson, what have I tried to instill in you over the years? Before you read whatever is written in that note, what can one deduce from the outside? Put the brain cells to work, man!"

I found myself doing as he suggested and, indeed, it did seem second nature, when he put it like that.

I picked up the paper by one corner and held it up to the light. I turned it this way and that, then held it up to my face, so that I could smell it. Finally, I replaced it where I had found it on my desk.

"Other than that it was written by a woman of some means and taste and that she was either frightened or in a hurry—and possibly both, I can tell you nothing. Except that her name is most probably Nana Kane."

Holmes clapped his hands together in delight and gave one of his mirthless laughs.

"Capital, old fellow! And how did you arrive at those deductions?"

"Ah well," I said, childishly pleased to have gained his approval. "The writing paper is of the highest quality to the touch and the water mark is of a top of the range brand of stationery. The handwriting is uncertain, indicating a flurried state of mind. And then, of course,"—I gave him a conspiratorial smile—"the whole thing reeks of Nana Kane's perfume."

I waited, rather like Mike, for a pat on the head. I should have known better.

Instead, Holmes simply said—

"Aren't you going to read what it has to say?"

Collapse of smug party. I unfolded the paper . . .

"My sister is about to do something terrible. I just know it. Please meet me at my apartment this evening at 8 o'clock. 75 Flamingo Street, Apt. 13a. I'm counting on you"

It was signed—

Anna

"You see, Watson, you made the mistake of coming to your conclusion based on too few facts."

Holmes seemed to be aware of the contents of the note without needing to read it.

"You were correct—but only up to a point. The notepaper is certainly expensive but is it not an odd shape? Observe the top edge. A portion of the paper has been cut off and the mark of the scissors is clearly visible. The paper almost certainly belongs to Nana Kane, as you deduced, but sister Anna has 'adapted' it for her own use. She wishes to separate herself—but only partially. The perfume is also Nana's distinctive fragrance but have we not detected traces of it on her sister, too?

"Then there is the question of the handwriting. Hurried? Perhaps. But there is something more at work here, old fellow. I have made some small study of handwriting, as you will doubtless recall. It is the expression of the writer's soul. This writing is artificial in the extreme, an effort of will. I would wager that, could we lay it side by side with Nana Kane's it would be the mirror opposite. Indicative of this woman's struggle not to be her troubled sibling. But by so doing she is finding difficulty in defining herself.

"Oh, and one other minor point . . . the slight traces of chlorine suggest that your trusty *chatelaine* received and almost certainly read the missive."

At least this part of Holmes's theory was conclusively proved as we left the building.

"Such a *polite* young lady, Mr. W.—not like so many of those you see today, prancing around in next to nothing, showing everything they've got. I do hope you can help her. Funny place for her to live, though, I should have thought . . ."

Whatever else she should have thought was lost

in the Corvette going through its heavy breathing routine before deciding to depart.

"And where are we headed, my dear fellow?"

"I thought we might treat ourselves to the movies . . ."

EIGHT

"Darling, do you want me to put the glass down *before* I move over to the window? Or wouldn't it be better if I moved towards the window, *then* looked at the glass, paused and then came back and put it down?"

"Whatever you're most comfortable with, darling."

"You see, I could be remembering the times when drink had come between me and the man I loved and I could have a wistful little smile there. It worked so well in *Say Hello to Goodbye* . . ."

"Yes, darling, I'm sure it did and I must remember to catch it on late night cable but this isn't *about* the man you loved. This is about three great ladies of the silver screen meeting years later—and one of them turns out to be a serial killer of old movie stars."

"So you think put the glass down *first,* darling?"

"I don't care *when* you put it or *where* you put it. In fact, Props, get rid of the God damn glass!"

"Yes, darling—I think that's best. I remember now, I had terrible trouble with a glass in *Empty Wives—Empty Lives* . . ."

"And empty *seats*." This last said semi-*sotto voce*.

". . . that stupid cameraman Marlene used to swear by lit the scene so that, what with the glare of the glass on my diamonds, it looked as though I had these terrible *bags* under my eyes."

"He should try lighting you now." Also under the breath but loud enough for Holmes and I to hear.

We were standing on the back lot—which also looked suspiciously like the front lot and possible the *whole* lot—at Superior Studios. A name coined by someone with a marked inferiority complex and a wicked sense of humor. It deserved its tag of "independent" since it was so small and inconspicuous it must have been one of the best kept secrets in Santa Monica. No burly gate-keeper demanding ID. No gate-keeper. Only the red light over the door indicated one of two things and, on balance and considering the time of day, I was inclined to reckon on it signifying a film studio. When it blinked off, we had shimmered in.

In one corner of the room was a partial set meant to indicate a down-at-the-heel residential hotel. Around the table three women were seated and, if they were enjoying the proceedings, that was the second best kept secret today. One of them was Linda Grace—the party of the first part in the unscripted off camera dialogue we'd just been listening to. She had gone back to studying her script and appeared satisfied that she had made a significant contribution to the proceedings.

The director seemed to feel otherwise. He was what you might call one of the old school. Tweed suit to give him that English look, even though the heat in here was in the upper 80s. Rimless eyeglasses on a chain. Thinning hair suitable for running despairing fingers through. School of Cecil B. De Mille. Sometime movie martinet but not any time recent. The whole production looked as though it had been put together in a thrift store and a cut price thrift store at that. If Nicky Parmentieri was bankrolling it, he had about as much riding on it as he would on a single turn of his roulette wheel.

The only exception to the general cheesiness were the ladies.

Now that I looked more closely, I could recognize the other two.

One was a professional blonde with distinctive candyfloss hair, so teased and sprayed she could have had half of Kane's aviary perched inside without anyone being any the wiser. When B-pictures were on their last legs, Edie Hatton had been on hers. Sassy secretary or aging hatcheck girl, she always had a wisecrack for the dumb cop or the executive with a poker up his ass. She'd made many a lemon palatable for the few minutes she was on the screen but I hadn't seen her for years, except in reruns. She hadn't aged well but then there hadn't been much to spoil in the looks department. She was now buffing her nails, as if they were an art form. After the nuclear holocaust we'd be left with two forms of life—the cockroach and Edie Hatton.

Agnes Winters was a different matter. She'd played great ladies in the style of Ethel Barrymore or Gladys Cooper in comedies of manners. That was in the days when there were manners to have comedies about. Tall, thin and patrician, she'd looked down many a mean lorgnette at a hapless hero. "Do I understand you wish to marry my daughter, young man?" Lady Bracknell with a Boston accent. Now she was a thin carbon copy of that *grande dame*. She looked as though the breeze from the clapper board would blow her away. Until it did—and until the director made his mind up what to do next—she sat there quietly crocheting and doing a crossword puzzle.

The whole scene brought a whole lot of memories flood without. The kid sneaking into the local movie house back home without paying, as someone else was leaving. Spooning—yes, we actually called it that!—in the back row with a girl whose face insisted on invading my dreams even now. Why couldn't the script we call Life be as predictable as the ones we paid good money to see? Or sometimes didn't pay.

There was also something indescribably sad about the whole set-up. Here were these ladies—pieces of living nostalgia—being brought together one last time and paid peanuts, so that some cheapskate producer could wring out the few last drops of sentiment from the handful of people who would ever get to see the schlock movie this promised to be.

The only person who didn't seem to understand the scenario was Linda Grace. Today she was an amalgam of her two goddess heroines. The eyes, circled in mascara to express permanent surprise, were pure 1940s Bette Davis but without Davis's intelligence. One more circle and Linda would only have needed a raccoon coat to complete the picture. The chalky complexion and the boldly-defined mouth were a curtsey to Joan Crawford. The wardrobe—clearly her own—was a mixture of the two and I'm sure, if I'd studied it more closely, there would have been hints of Susan Hayward, Gloria Grahame, *et al.* in there somewhere. The woman was a walking exhibition of "Hollywood—the Golden Years."

And she was having the time of her life. Or she was until her director spoiled it.

He was perched on a stool a few feet away from me, making a snack of his fingernail. The rest of his fingers suggested he'd been dining well recently. At that moment Linda sailed up to him. Why she had chosen to wear a fur stole in an indoor location wasn't entirely clear but she had.

"Jonty, darling," she cooed, leaning over and into him in a way I recalled well. It was a ploy that I'm sure had proved consistently effective in the not-too-recent past but it was lost on Jonty. "Jonty? Don't you think it would be better if, instead of my sitting there with those two old ladies, I were to make an entrance and *find* them there, living out their poor lonely lives? After all, darling, I *am* the star of this picture and my fans will expect . . ."

If she could be Davis and Crawford, then Jonty showed that he could do a fair De Mille, when there was an audience present and he'd had it up to here.

"*Fans?* Any fans you ever had would be as old as Lady Windermere's!"

She was clearly stricken but she took it in her stride.

"You know I've been resting, darling. This is my come-back picture."

"Listen, sister, to come back you have to have been there in the first place."

"Now, listen to me, you decrepit little fag . . ."—"decrepit" clearly hurt—"*I* was big when you were running errands and giving blow jobs to C-picture directors." We were now getting a whiff of the lady's true origins. Equally, it was plain that someone who had never had

142

his name above the title and now never would was determined to play *his* one big scene to the hilt.

"Big? By the time you came along all the greats were gone. There was no big—except as in budget. Everything and everybody was small. TV actors with a lot of hot air pumped in them. Hollywood was over, baby. You make out you're some latter-day Davis or Crawford. You couldn't hold an eyebrow pencil to them! And this piece of shit you call your comeback. A tax write-off, if ever I saw one. It'll finish up on cut-price video being watched by a bunch of ga-ga senior citizens in a twilight home, who'll think you're Mabel Normand or Lilian Gish. I'd rather be directing a tampon commercial . . ."

"Then I suggest you go and find one."

A man's voice interrupted his soliloquy and out of the shadows stepped Nicky Parmentieri.

"You disappoint me, Jonty. This was meant to be a happy ship. You may not realize it but you were one of my childhood heroes. Saturday morning TV watching Hopalong Cassidy reruns. 'The part of Skeeter was played by John "Jonty" Evans.' I was paying off a debt, Jonty. Well, consider it paid. Good day to you."

There was total silence on the set. There was something about the way Nicky had spoken that ended the discussion.

Jonty pulled the shreds of his tattered dignity

about him and threw down the script he had been holding with as much defiance as he could muster.

"If that's the way you want it, Nicky. Cut me my check and I'm out of here."

"No check, Jonty. But if you want to discuss it, there are other ways we can pay you off."

Jonty apparently *didn't* want to discuss them. A moment later there was the boom of the studio door closing.

The ensuing silence was broken by Linda, giving her best performance of the day.

"What a *schmuck*! De Mille never spoke to me like that, nor Wilder, nor Cukor . . ."

Probably because you never *worked* with any of them, I thought.

"OK, everybody, it's a wrap," Nicky called. Since everything and everybody in the place was clearly bought and paid for by him, nobody was about to argue. The arc lights snapped off and in the comparative gloom I saw Edie give her nails a final buff and Agnes put away her crochet. They'd both been here a time or two before and would be again, the Good Lord willing. Another day, another dollar—minus ten percent agent's fee, of course.

"You OK, baby doll?"

Nicky had his arm around Linda's shoulders and was now leading her towards the door.

"I was big, Nicky. You know that. *Angels Don't*

Cry grossed bigger than anything its first week in Trenton, New Jersey. And Cincinnati . . ."

"Don't let them get to you, baby. They're assholes."

That seemed to placate her.

"Right, Nicky. They're *all* assholes." She snuggled up to him. "And anyway, we've got plans. Right, Nicky?"

He disengaged himself slightly, as he pushed open the heavy door. As they passed through it, I heard him say—

"Right, baby doll. We got plans. We got plans but they ain't nobody's business but ours. OK?"

"OK, Nicky."

The door boomed behind them.

"Well, I came to see Linda Grace and didn't exchange a word with her."

"And yet you still learned something, did you not, old fellow?"

"I learned that she was an even worse actress than I'd remembered and that she and Nicky had 'plans.' Yet she's supposedly married to Kane. Where does he fit into all this, Holmes?"

"I don't think they intend that he should and I doubt very much that he cares either way—as long as he ends up with the Bird."

"Trophy Bird outranks trophy bride? But who's *got* the goddam Bird?"

145

This whole business was giving me the feeling that I was chasing my tail every bit as much as Mike does in the dog days of summer.

Then I fixed Holmes with my best beady stare.

"I've got a feeling you've known from the beginning and you're just not saying. Am I right?"

"Watson, I am, as you will have observed, in a rather peculiar position. Certain of my natural abilities are enhanced, others strangely absent. I am not permitted to tell you anything you cannot discover for yourself. I may prompt your line of thought and, I imagine, *in extremis*, protect your safety. Don't ask me how I know this, because I am at a loss to know the reason myself, but the lines of demarcation are quite clear to me. It is useless to press me further. Let us, therefore, review what we know . . ."

"Very well," I said, a little huffily. Nonetheless, somehow I knew that what he said was true. "We have one benighted Bird. Kane says it was stolen and Anna Kane confirms that her sister Nana was the one who stole it and gave it away.

"Supposition One. Nana lied to her sister for some reason about stealing the Bird. Kane, for some reason, is *pretending* it's missing and has it all the time. Now, why would he do that? He can't have it insured since he's not supposed to have it in the first place, so we're not looking at an insurance scam here. Is he using the 'theft' as a way of getting back at Parmentieri for upsetting his drug business?

"Supposition Two. Nana *did* steal the Bird and gave it to her boyfriend, Nicky. Since she can't prove it either way and the only possible witness, old White Suit, has gone to that Great Dry Cleaner in the Sky, Nicky can deny having received it. Maybe he has a customer in mind—another Kane who'll come across with the readies, so that he can gloat in private. Lots of people would like to stick it to Kane. And Nicky keeps a nice piece of change he doesn't have to divvy up with the Pomonas. Possible.

"Supposition Three. Kane never *did* get the original Bird back after he had it copied. He got another and better copy and that's the copy Nicky has nestling among his underwear in his bottom drawer. Mallory still has the real thing. If so, he's stuck between a rock and a hard place and shouldn't start reading any serial stories."

"Excellent, Watson. You have, however, omitted one other possibility. Mallory has already sold the Bird to that someone else and *none* of them has it. Perhaps the Bird has already flown the nest?

"Perhaps we shall learn more at our next port of call. What did you say the address was—Flamingo Street?"

NINE

Flamingo Street was precisely as you would expect a thoroughfare with a name like that to be. Built in the 1920s when movies made up for not being able to talk by beguiling the innocent eye with lavish sets that had all the solidity of plasterboard, this was a mean street in more ways than one.

Pink stucco as far as the eye could see, it must have once beamed hopefully in the California sun. Now time and industrialized weather had caused its makeup to run and several generations of transient tenants on the way up, down and, all too often, but had not bothered to cover the acne in its complexion. As if to symbolize all this, the plaster flamingo set in *bas-relief* on the wall of the corner house had a broken beak.

No. 75 was a wooden three-storied structure now divided up as a rooming house. Seven tenants had their names next to a series of buzzers and the most recent-looking name by far—indicated by her distinctive business card—was "Anna K. Adam." I pressed her bell and an angry hornet noise released the front door. Holmes, Mike and I walked in and the door swung to behind us with a great deal more alacrity than it had shown in opening. The mouse was in the trap.

As it did, the door of one of the ground floor apartments opened a crack and an eagle female eye appeared behind the security chain. No home is complete, it would appear, without a Guardian Gryppe.

"Don't know why she bothers. Never here. Waste of money, you ask me."

The door closed again. Perhaps the whole thing was a hologram triggered by the lock. This *was* Hollywood after all.

"Up here, Jack."

Anna Kane/Adam lived at the very top of the house in what I suppose a real estate agent would call a "cozy studio." All I know is that, if it had been any smaller, she could have put it in her purse and taken it with her.

It wasn't a nest—it was a perch. There was no sign that she had made any attempt to settle in. Her few possessions seemed to lie there rather than seek a home of their own. I could see precisely what her Cyclops neighbor meant. More to the point, Anna could see me seeing.

As she closed the door behind us—Mike and me, as far as she was concerned—she handed me the shot glass she was holding in her other hand.

"Jack Daniel's. Right? All private detectives drink Jack Daniel's." She picked up its twin from the kitchen table, which also happened to be the sitting room table *and* the bedside table.

Since I like people to keep their illusions—and

because it had been a thirsty sort of day—I took it and raised it in a toast.

"May your bluebird of happiness never spit in your eye!" It was something I'd learned at my mother's knee and I'd changed it only slightly for present company.

My attempt at levity was entirely lost on the girl. She downed the drink in one—a course of action not to be recommended in the normal run of events. In the first place it's an insult to good bourbon and in the second, it makes the neophyte cough. She held on to me until the fit passed and I reflected that women seemed to be making a habit of using me as a hitching post since this case began. It was a comment more than a complaint. I've known worse experiences.

"It's Nana." The baby browns were turned on me full wattage. "She called me last night in a terrible state. It's that bird, I swear it is. She says it's evil and corrupts everyone it touches. And then started rambling about someone needing to destroy those who have possessed it before it possesses us all.

"Jack, I'm deathly afraid she has convinced herself she is that person. The Avenging Angel. I think losing the Bird has turned her mind. She has to divert the guilt she feels in some other direction. You *must* help me, Jack. There is no one else . . ."

Now why was there something in her tone

that reminded me of Linda Grace an hour or so before? Or was it just that *everyone* in Tinsel Town talked like a character in a cheap melodrama?

This slight hiatus gave me time to check out what my companions were up to. Not that they could wander far in this matchbox. There wasn't room to swing a medium-sized cat, let alone a chunky mongrel. In fact, by the time Anna had fetched her drink she had walked through Holmes twice. He, I noticed, was examining the few clothes hanging on a single rack in the corner of the room, while Mike was truffle hunting under the single divan bed.

"Think, Jack, think. Who could have it? It has to be Nicky, doesn't it?"

"What about Mallory?" I said before I had time to edit my thoughts.

I saw Holmes turn and look in our direction but he was looking at her and not me.

The merest shadow seemed to cross her eyes and then she shook her head decisively. "That obscene man? Never. He'd be too scared to cross my father. No, it has to be Nicky. He's the only one left.

"I want you to go and see him, Jack. See him and warn him that if he doesn't give the Bird back, it will kill him, just as it killed Brent Perlman and . . ."

"And?"

"The dozens of others over the centuries."

Somehow I didn't think that was what she had started out to say. And somehow I wanted to get out of that claustrophobic little room.

"Let me sleep on it," I said and patted her hand. Honest to God, I found myself patting her hand! Bing Crosby as Father O'Malley in *Going My Way*. If my friends could see me now—always supposing I *had* any friends.

"You have to understand Nana . . ." If she noticed my Freudian slip, she showed no sign of it. *What* Freudian slip?—". . . that your father is my client. Whatever you think of him and whatever I may have come to think of him," I added generously, "I am professionally committed to fulfill my responsibilities to him first and foremost. But you may be sure that I will do everything in my power to protect your sister's interests at the same time."

Where did I get this stuff? I was making my "professional commitment" sound like the Hippocratic Oath, though to my ears it came out sounding more like the Hypocritic Oath.

"I understand about being a professional, I really do. And I know you'll do all you can. You're a good man, Jack. And I haven't met too many."

Then, to my surprise and slight concern, she quickly kissed my cheek. Where *was* this interview going? I looked around for moral

153

support but both of my good buddies were looking pointedly the other way.

"I'm glad we had this chance to get to know each other a little better—just the three of us."

"The *three* of us?" I knew she couldn't see *Holmes*. I didn't want to even contemplate that she'd meant *Mike* . . . and I couldn't detect a crevice even Petit could have curled up in. We were alone.

"You, me—and Jack Daniel's." She moved carefully in the direction of the bottle. She and good old Jack had been reminiscing over old times well before I arrived. I decided to leave them to it. I had enough problems for one day. Besides, entering into a relationship of a personal nature in the presences of a ghost and an adopted, unlicensed dog would probably mean my badge. I was also helped by recalling Dorothy Parker's deathless line about one more drink and she'd be under the host. In this case—the hostess. Literature has its uses.

I raised an apparently reluctant hand in an "I'm-doing-this-more-for-your-own-good-than-mine" gesture. It must have looked pathetic. At least, it would have done to a lady who was half-way sober, which this one was not. Whatever happened to the Little Miss Muffet who had sat on her tuffet in my office not too long ago? *Ou sont les demoiselles d'antan*? Well might you ask.

As I walked down the stairs with Mike at my

154

heels, I heard her call after me—"Sleep on it, Jack—but don't sleep too late! *Tempus fugit.*" Now, could someone drunk have quoted Virgil?

I couldn't quote him when sober.

Holmes put it into words when were once more back in the office.

"As I have had cause to observe more than once, Watson, the motives of women are inscrutable."

"Which woman in particular did you have in mind on this occasion?"

Instead of answering, he continued, seeming to speak as to himself rather than to me—

"One should always look for a possible alternative and provide against it. It is the first rule of criminal investigation."

Then, shaking himself out of his reverie—

"Her apartment reminded me of nothing so much as the 'safe houses' I used to keep in London. I had five of them at one time. I would enter as one person and leave as another. Did you notice the clothes, old fellow? No, of course, you could not. She gave you no opportunity, did she? All of them still had the shop labels attached. None of them had been worn.

"A bad mistake, old fellow. Disguises should always be well worn. But then, perhaps she does not intend them to be worn. Perhaps today was their first and last performance.

"You observed, of course, that all the dresses

had long sleeves—a point to which I have called your attention on several occasions?"

"So both sisters suffer from hypothermia? Probably runs in the family. The old man sits and stews himself in a casserole."

Holmes raised a disgusted eyebrow.

"Needle marks, Watson—needle marks! The long sleeves are to cover those all-too-evident puncture marks that give away the habitual drug taker. The lady was not only intoxicated but also under some narcotic influence, almost certainly cocaine. A dangerous combination and one I have personally always avoided. That, I surmise, is the cause of her otherwise inexplicable mood swings.

"That you *should* have noticed but there was one other item which you were most decidedly *not* intended to see . . ."

"Which was?"

Without answering, he continued . . .

"Tucked away behind the clothes rack with its face to the wall—but which my present unorthodox condition allowed me to see, nonetheless, was a rather unusual portrait . . ."

"Whose?"

"The portrait was of Osgood Kane, painted by a competent studio hack—about thirty years ago, I would judge. However, someone had defaced it in a most obscene manner, until it resembled nothing so much as the one Dorian Gray kept locked away in his attic in our friend Oscar Wilde's notorious story. Oh yes, and I believe Mike also has something to offer us . . ."

I realized that Mike had been suspiciously quiet on the return journey and looked over to the basket I kept for him in the corner. Needless to say, he only occupies it when he is up to no good or wishes to remain out of the public eye of this private eye until some misdemeanor is discovered. He lay there contentedly chewing the corner of a piece of paper.

I retrieved it and smoothed it out on my desk, avoiding the soggy end as far as possible. It was an account from a well-known firm of Hollywood wig makers and it read—

1 LADIES' BLONDE (MID)— CHIGNON STYLE

I found myself blurting out the thought that had been edging its way further and further forward in my mind.

"Holmes—is this woman really Nana Kane *pretending* to be her sister, Anna? She was certainly behaving differently from yesterday. If I didn't know better, I'd say she was starting to come on to me."

"I assume you mean she found you sexually attractive? Naturally, old fellow, I defer to your experience of women in three separate continents—although strictly speaking, India is only a *sub*-continent—but that is a technicality.

"No, Watson, Anna Kane and Nana Kane are two quite distinct *personae*. They have nothing in common but a coincidence of birth. In attempting to anticipate their actions, it would be as well not to ignore that fact.

"Women are never to be entirely trusted—not even the best of them. The most winning woman I ever knew was hanged for poisoning three little children for their insurance money."

"But how do we get to the bottom of this?" I asked. "I feel we may be standing on the edge of a precipice here. If Anna is right, her sister may be about to embark on a killing spree. We must *do* something!"

"And, indeed, we shall, my dear fellow. But first I suggest we should pay the call we should have made at the very beginning of this bizarre affair. We should mine the mother lode."

"The mother lode?"

"Watson, I venture to suggest that a visit to the first Mrs. Osgood Kane is indicated."

"But I haven't the faintest idea how to find her, Holmes. I hardly think a call to Kane and 'Oh, by the way, which loony bin did you lock your wife up in?' is going to do the trick."

And then I thought—no, but I know what will. I reached for the phone.

"Morrie. Is that you?"

TEN

SUNNYVALE
A Heaven of a Haven

Who writes this stuff! Nonetheless, the etched marble sign communicated serious money. The kind of money that said you can leave your loved one here and forget about them—as long as you don't forget about the check. All major credit cards honored. Standing orders preferred.

Pitch in a little more—say another couple of grand a day—and they'll decorate your loved one's suite so that the Dear Disoriented or Beloved Befuddled don't even know they've left home. Which saves you having to leave yours.

We wove our way around flower beds that were hand painted and lawns that were clearly clipped every hour on the hour by a team of gnomes with nail scissors. Ah, unspoiled Nature—you can't beat it!

It was the morning of the following day. The good weather had decided to break and was giving us a trailer. The dark clouds would be along in the next reel but, meanwhile, a little thunder (in Dolby sound) was rolling around the hills and any moment you knew the ominous theme music would creep in, warning you to get ready for the Big Finale, when "all" would be revealed.

I had awakened early from a nightmare in which all the characters seemed to morph into each other with disconcerting regularity.

"Oh, I *do* hate birds!" said Quentin Mallory. He then proceeded to remove his face but when he handed it to Petit, it had turned into the Borgia Bird, gleaming as if straight from the furnace. The little man juggled it painfully.

"Christ, that's hot!"

"No need for formality, pipsqueak. You may simply call me 'Sir.' "

"Excuse me, 'Sir,' but do you have something for me?"

Petit had vanished, his place taken by Nana Kane, who was dressed like one of the dancers in the Birdland cabaret and carrying a mask on a stick. Every so often she would put the mask up to her face, when she became Anna for a moment. Nana-Anna-Nana-Anna.

"Not known at this address," shouted Mallory but his voice seemed to come from far away. Now I could see that he was growing even taller like Alice and his upper body was already lost in the clouds. "Sorry I can't stay but I have an assignation with Caesar's wife . . ."

"More like the Queen of Tarts," said a new voice.

I turned to see Nicky sitting cross-legged on the

floor and playing solitaire with a deck of cards. Except that although it was clearly Nicky, he was now a small boy in short trousers. He turned up the last card in his hand and threw it on top of the pile.

I could see that it had the face of the Devil on it.

"Shit!" said Nicky.

"Shit!" I heard myself say, as Mike leapt on to my bed and gave my face a vigorous lick. It was his early morning ritual to let me know he wanted to go out or I could take the consequences.

I took the easy option—and dealt with the consequences later.

By nine the wagons were rolling . . .

The entrance hall of Sunnyvale was Carrera marble, the real thing not veneer. I know because Holmes told me. He seemed quite impressed. The receptionist who greeted us was also the real thing. And I didn't need Holmes to tell me that. It was proved without the shadow of a doubt when she bent forward to check the register and I found myself poised on the edge of the Grand Canyon. Holmes's "Watson!" caused me to step back from the brink in the nick of time.

She was sorry, she said, when she had returned the vertical, but there was no record of an anticipated visitor for Guest Eloise. "Guest" Eloise. No "Mrs. Kane." No family name. This was the Hotel Incognito, where you checked in until you checked out for good.

Things began to look up when I explained that I was working for Mr. Kane himself and showed his signature—the rest of the check carefully obscured by my P.I. license. Mr. Kane—repetition always works in communication, I find—had urgent business and would most certainly not wish to hear that his special operative's inquiries had been impeded by . . . She got the point and floated an enigmatic little smile in my general direction.

She must have pressed a buzzer under the desk without my noticing. Hardly surprising, since my attention was almost entirely focused above the Mason-Dixon Line.

I was made aware (by a small cough) of the presence of a second person at my elbow. She was a slightly older woman in a white nurse's uniform and if Reception was the siren song, she was the soothing lullaby. Sharon Stone for the Receptionist. Susan Sarandon for the Nurse.

Susan escorted us down more marble halls and through what appeared to be a recreation area that had a Twilight Zone air about it. Men and women of all ages sat around in designer track suits watching TV sets with the sound turned low or turning the pages of picture magazines in slow motion. You could sense that the activities were purely incidental to their sitting there in this final waiting room. I had a vision of the transmission of *I Love Lucy* suddenly being interrupted as a number came up on all the screens and one of the patients got to his or her feet and marched zombie-like to the door. All eyes would follow them for a brief moment, until Lucy and Desi resumed their antics and the eyes swiveled back to the only reality they now knew.

Down a carpeted corridor now and past a series of doors with homely little ceramic name plates—"DAWN," "HARRY," "SIMONE," and finally, "ELOISE."

Susan knocked gently, opened the door and stepped back to allow me to enter.

"Someone to see you, Eloise." Then to me— "I'll be back in five minutes. That should give you plenty of time." She also gave me a twin to the small smile I'd had from Sharon. A moment later I could see why.

Eloise Kane was dressed for afternoon tea. Presumably at one of the Queen's Garden Parties. She wore a long floaty kind of dress, little white gloves and a large picture hat. Was this what gave Nana the idea—some childhood memory of unhappy families?

Her face, when she turned it in our direction, was chalk white with powder, a pallor broken only by a slash of red where her lipstick had made occasional and erratic contact with her mouth. But the voice was a complete contrast—

soft and modulated. A great lady welcoming her cherished guests.

"You are naughty, being so late. We were just going to start without you."

Then I saw who "we" were.

A small card table was laid for tea but the crockery was minute, clearly taken from a doll's house. Eloise returned to the task that had been occupying her before our arrival—pouring nothing from an empty teapot into empty cups. There were three chairs at the table—an ordinary one for her and two chairs big enough for the two dolls that occupied them.

They were cheap unisex dolls, the sort you can buy at any Five and Dime store but she had dressed them beautifully—one in pink and the other in blue—and the clothes looked handmade. I would have bet a fair amount that she had made them herself.

The pouring done, she looked up at me and seemed to look through me. The expression in those washed-out blue eyes said without the need for further explanation that the lady was out to lunch and wouldn't be coming back for any more meals.

"Oh, but what must you think of me? You haven't been properly introduced." She picked up the girl doll and manipulated the hand, so that it was held out to be shaken. Rather self-consciously, I did so.

"This is Nana. And she's going to be very well known when she grows up. Aren't you, Nana?"

I felt a chill, as Eloise spoke for the "child" in what she presumably thought was a ventriloquist's voice.

"Yes, Mommy."

The doll was put back in her seat and the boy doll picked up.

"And this is my little boy"—A puzzled look crossed her face. "I'm sorry but I can't remember his name. I don't see him very often. He's a very busy little man, aren't you?"

Again the grotesque child's voice, a little gruffer this time.

"Yes, Mommy. Very busy."

Then some troubling wellspring of emotion seemed to bubble up inside her. Suddenly she snatched both the dolls and hugged them to her bosom. Her eyes were now totally opaque and she began to chant—

"N-n-n-nan-n-n-na."

I exchanged glances with Holmes and he made a slight shake of the head, indicating that we could hope for nothing more. As if on cue the door opened and Susan entered. She didn't seem unduly surprised by what she found but went across to Eloise and, putting a comforting arm around her shoulders, began to speak to her quietly.

As Holmes and I left the room, she gave us a

quick glance that seemed to say—"Satisfied?"

In Reception Sharon had fortunately gone off duty. Her place had been taken by a Julia Roberts clone, who looked as though, taken in regular doses, she could be equally lethal. Fortunately, she was reading a magazine and posed no immediate problem. We made the outside world in safety.

As we crossed to the parking lot, soft electronic chimes began to play. If this had been a monastery or convent—which from the atmosphere it might well be—I would have assumed a call to prayer. As it was, I guessed a call to lunch.

So this was the way the world ended? Personally, I'd prefer to go out with a bang on the back of the head in some dark alley, rather than with a whimper in some sedated prelude to The Big Sleep. But, then the choice was so rarely ours to make.

On the drive back I took the coast road.

Miklos Rozsa as Max Steiner—or whoever was in charge of the orchestrations—had added a little more percussion and timpani to go with the flashes of lightning that were beginning to light up the hills in a free Wagnerian *son et lumière* that would cost thousands in a studio.

Somehow it seemed to underline my mood. Being in Eloise Kane's presence, however briefly, had depressed me profoundly. All that money

166

could buy—and yet nothing. Rather like this case. A lot of activity but no forward movement that I could detect.

Perhaps a little music would help cheer me up. I put in one of my favorite cassettes—a rock 'n roll compilation. As my luck would have it, first up was Elvis complaining that, since his baby had left him, he'd found a new place to dwell. It was at the end of Lonesome Street and called Heartbreak Hotel. Try Sunnyvale, kiddo, I thought. At least it *sounds* cheerful.

Then I noticed Holmes was tapping those long, thin fingers on the dashboard in time to the music.

"I wouldn't have thought this was your kind of music, Holmes."

"It has a certain primitive charm, Watson, I must admit. What is the name of the artiste?"

"Elvis Presley."

"Oh, dear me, no." He smiled as he shook his head. "Edouard De Reske, Enrico Caruso, Fydor Chaliapin . . . but *Elvis Presley!* No, my dear fellow, I'm afraid he will have to do better than that if he is to be successful."

Since there was nothing I could usefully add, we drove along in silence for a little while, as the no-hope singer finished his dirge. I switched the tape off.

"A wasted journey, I'm afraid?"

"Depressing, I grant you. The human condition

is at best a precarious one and some degree of tragedy, great or small, lurks behind every façade that we pass. But *wasted?* I think not."

"But the woman plays with dolls and thinks they are her children."

"Yes, but she plays with *two* dolls—not three.

"A long run for a short slide—as I have heard you say, Watson. But that slide carries us that much closer to the finish line. Or am I mixing my metaphors?"

ELEVEN

Back in the office the red light on my phone was flashing to show I had messages. This is a fairly recent innovation for me. For years I had espoused the Dale Carnegie thesis that to make friends and influence people you had perforce to meet them face to face. But when some of those faces seem intent on getting *in* your face, then a little prior screening seems to be called for. An insult on the phone is infinitely preferable to an altercation in an alley in the scheme of things.

The first was from our Oxford Charlie Chan . . .

"My dear Mr. Watson. I do hope when this dreadful affair has run its course, we can sit down and break bread—or even share a bowl of rice—together. It is becoming quite embarrassing. Here am I with my unhappy band of pilgrims, who have come all this way with blood lust raging through their veins in pursuit of their holy relic and on each occasion they are frustrated by finding someone has preempted them.

"I ask you, Mr. Watson, is the severing of a deceased digit adequate recompense for a trained assassin? And then today's little fiasco . . . I apologize in advance for the theatrical touch my lieutenant Weng Lu insisted on adding but he felt a pressing need to contribute *something*. It's the artist in him, you know. It would have been a loss of face otherwise. No pun intended.

"The natives are getting restless, my dear fellow. I really would urge you to redouble your efforts. I'd hate to see you turn from hunter to hunted."

The second was Anna Kane . . . a very frightened Anna Kane . . .

"Jack. It's me, Anna. Why did you rush off like that? I had so much to say to you. Listen, Jack—I've just spoken to Nana and she's done something terrible again but she won't say what. I don't know which way to turn. Jack, can't you come round here?"

Then the call cut off abruptly. Or had someone at her end cut it off? And what could I do that Jack Daniel's couldn't do better and faster?

The third was Osgood Kane, asking for a progress report. The words were polite but, even through the distortion of the phone line and the voice box, there was an underlying edge to his tone. Since there was no progress to report, I felt no obligation to return his call in a hurry. I pressed the Recall button again.

The last call got my serious attention.

The voice was familiar but I couldn't place it for the moment.

"This is Dwight . . ."

Dwight?

Then the caller seemed to realize an explanation was needed.

"Petit. Mallory calls me Petit. You've got to come here right away. I know I should call the cops but I want to do the right thing. Mallory liked you. And you treated *me* OK. You'll know what to do. *Please!*"

There was the sound of an open line.

"You heard that, Holmes?" He nodded. " 'Liked.' Past tense."

"I'm very much afraid that what we have here, old fellow, are the elements of Greek tragedy. And if so, then events are moving toward their predestined end.

"However, we must see what we can do to moderate them. I suggest we waste no further time."

We clattered, drifted and padded down the stairs and across Mrs. Plack's newly washed lobby floor, causing the good lady to lean on her mop with her favorite martyred expression that said—"Some people!" For once I agreed with her, though in a rather different context. Some people, indeed.

Mallory's showroom had a dark, deserted look, like a stage set after the closing night of the play. Something about it tells you that not only the actors but the characters themselves have moved on and won't be coming back until they find another author.

Nor did the weather help. The rain hadn't arrived but the sky was growing steadily darker and a wind was rising, coming in from the ocean with a salty dampness you could taste. The darkness was bleaching out the color, turning everything into a contrasty *film noir*.

Oscar Wilde used to say that life merely imitated art and usually did it rather badly. In Hollywood life imitated the movies. You just had to learn to recognize which ones.

I tried the door handle. As I expected—locked. Then there was a scuttling noise from within, like a pack of mice—if mice hunt in packs—and then the sound of several locks and bolts and chains being unfastened.

The face of Petit peered past the final security chain. But only his height-challenged stature reminded me of the little man I had seen on my last visit. Gone was the chippy assertiveness and the pugnacious stance. Instead, I was looking at a badly frightened wizened child.

Petit slipped the last chain and stood back to let me in. The moment we were past him, I heard the barricades being hurriedly replaced.

"In there." There being the work room.

Holmes, Mike and I moved through the show-room. Nothing appeared to have been disturbed. It was the same jumble of styles and eras that I'd seen before. Anyone but Mallory or Petit would need a road map to find what they were looking for.

There was a kind of sensory overload about the place. There were just too many images to take in, so effectively you saw nothing. And yet . . . was it my imagination or was there something different today that I was missing? Before I could stop to think about it, Petit had hurried me into the inner sanctum.

Here it was a very different story. The place had been ransacked—turned over by someone who wanted to find something and wanted you to know that he wanted to find something—if you know what I mean. There were no prizes for guessing what.

Drawers were pulled out and their contents littered the floor—moulds, instruments, files. I found myself crunching over something on the floor. When I looked down, I saw I was walking on the fragments of ceramic birds. No wonder Petit was upset. There were years of work and loving care in those shards.

But, strangely, that didn't seem to be what was bothering him. When I looked up, the little man was standing at the far end of the room at the side of a large screen, the kind they use in hospitals to give a patient privacy in a public ward. Mike was standing by his side and peering behind it. Now, Mike is a dog with attitude but his present attitude was strictly ears and tail down.

I suddenly had a nasty premonition concerning what I was about to find . . .

Behind the screen was a long work bench, presumably one Petit used daily, and on it, stretched out as though taking an afternoon nap was Quentin Mallory. It had to be Mallory or two ordinary people laid end to end, occupying one of his suits.

His hands were folded primly over his stomach and to keep the mosquitoes at bay he had placed a white handkerchief over his face. On the beach or in a garden hammock it would have been an idyllic sight. In this context it was more than a little disturbing.

For one thing there was no reassuring rise and fall of his chest, no flutter of the handkerchief caused by the lips of the sleeper. I didn't need to be a coroner to know that this was an extinct antique dealer I was looking at.

I heard a low keening sound. To be accurate, I heard two. One was from Mike, whose tail was now firmly between his legs. The other was from Petit, who, I now saw, was standing by Mallory's covered face.

As I moved towards him, he suddenly whipped the cloth away, like a chef presenting his *specialité du jour*. At which point I nearly lost my breakfast and the combined meals of the past several days.

For Quentin Mallory no longer had a face. Somebody who had a handy way with a scalpel had neatly removed it. I also saw that I had been

174

correct in my supposition that his crowning glory was a hairpiece, since it was nestling cozily on top of his skull. I had heard of people being scalped but here was someone who had been defaced and his scalp left *in situ*.

Now, when the time comes for me to make my exit, I have to say that, all things considered, I'd prefer to meet my Maker face—as it were—to face. But perhaps at that time all normal bets are off. And, in any case, before I hastily replaced the cloth, I had time to observe that it wasn't a loss of face that had caused him to shuffle off to Buffalo.

Someone had drilled a neat bullet hole through Mallory's forehead, leaving him with a third eye through which he wouldn't be seeing a thing either.

"Watson," said Holmes's voice in my head, "I see you have discovered the cause of death. Would you be so good as to come over here? It would appear that our hyperactive oriental friends have been at work again."

I looked around but Holmes was nowhere to be seen. From which I deduced that he must have returned to the showroom. I made my way back there with Petit bringing up the rear. Mike decided to stay put well out of harm's way.

Holmes was standing in the midst of what looked like a battlefield. There was medieval armor, weaponry, banners. You could have staged a rerun of Agincourt with no trouble at all and had enough left over for a couple of small sieges.

There was also, now that I came to look more closely, a long row of kneeling terracotta figures. I remembered I'd seen something about them on a cable TV show. That's right. The Xian Warriors. Hundreds of years old but only unearthed in northern China in fairly recent times and now replicas were *de rigeur* in all the most pretentious gardens coast to coast.

Holmes was standing somewhere near the middle of the row and his thin hand pointed to the warrior nearest him. As I came closer, something in the pit of my stomach told me what I was about to see. And it was right.

One of the warriors was wearing Mallory's face like a Halloween mask. It had been put there and then lacquered in place. The pot of lacquer and a brush were at the statue's feet. Among the impassive faces of the line of Chinese chorus boys Mallory's deathly white grin stood out, as he took his final bow.

Well, it was certainly a memorable way to go, that had to be said for it.

Behind me there was a soft thud. I turned to see that Petit had fainted. The only consolation was that at least he hadn't had far to fall.

"I suppose it would be too much to ask for you to find your bodies the way decent ordinary

176

people do—stabbed in the library by the butler, dumped in a Dumpster by the Mob, swinging from a bellrope? No, you have to give us Baron Frankenstein's laboratory, complete with Igor over there. While we're here, perhaps you'd like to give us some idea of Coming Attractions? God knows how I'm going to do the paperwork on this one . . ."

McNulty seemed to have arrived almost before I'd put the phone down. Now the premises were discreetly sealed with the shop's CLOSED sign. But, to my surprise, there was no yellow crime scene tape and he hadn't filled the place with uniforms. In fact, apart from the police surgeon, who was now examining Mallory's body, he only had his regular sergeant in attendance.

McNulty soon made his thinking clear.

"I don't know if that little weasel Nicky is behind this one, too, but I sure ain't taking chances. We're piecing something together on his operation and if I move too soon, he'll be through the net and walking away whistling Dixie. Which I definitely don't want.

"Mallory's been mixed up with him somehow or other but a couple of things don't add up. If this is another execution, the bullet's in the wrong place. Back of the head is the friendly family way. Pow! *Ciao*! And it's the wrong kind of bullet. Nothing more than a .22, from the look of it. We call it the 'Lady's Special' in the trade.

177

Well, you don't need me to tell you that. And this stuff with the face. That's not the work of a pro—not unless we've got somebody who's thinking of retiring and taking up taxidermy.

"Anyway, *compadre mio*, I don't know what your interest in this guy is—and frankly, at this moment I don't *want* to know. So what I'm saying to you, nicely as I know how, is . . . for the next twenty-four hours it's the zipped lip. OK?"

"OK."

Which suited me just fine. Twenty-four hours was just about long enough for me to play out the scheme that was forming in what passes for my brain.

At that moment the medic came over, stripping off his gloves.

"As we thought, Lieutenant. Single shot from a .22 at close quarters. Somebody he knew, most probably, to get that close. No sign of a struggle. We'll sweep the place, of course, but the only thing I've found so far is this . . ."

He took a clear plastic evidence envelope from his apron pocket and handed it to McNulty, who held it up to the light.

"Looks like a single hair. Too long to be a man's. Blondish."

"*Mid*-blonde. Chignon Style." It was Holmes whispering in my head. "Come along, old fellow, there is nothing more we can do here and time is of the essence."

178

I told McNulty I'd keep in touch and he told me he'd keep in touch. And neither of us believed a word of it. All the same I had a shrewd suspicion he wouldn't be far away.

TWELVE

Flamingo Street hadn't looked like much when the sun was shining. In the rain its feathers looked positively bedraggled.

No. 75 seemed to have shrunk, as if it were pulling its shingles tighter around it to ward off the chill. It looked like nothing so much as a disgruntled garden bird waiting for the rain to stop so that it could move on to another anonymous perch.

There was no answer to Anna K. Adam's bell. Nor was there any "Anna K. Adam" business card in the slot any more. Just a fragment of scotch tape to show where it had been. I can't say I was entirely surprised.

I then pulled the trick that has always annoyed the hell out of me when I've lived in buildings like this. I rang all the bells in turn. Somebody would be stupid enough to press the release buzzer. They always had in *my* buildings.

No buzzer buzzed but the door did suddenly open a crack. There behind the security chain was an eagle eye I recognized from our last visit.

"Oh, it's you. Thought somebody would be round. Told you, didn't I? Always tell a fly-by-night. Get the money first, my motto."

"I wonder if I could see Miss Adam's room for a moment, madam? She said she'd leave something for me."

Quick thinking, Watson. They've got to get up pretty early . . .

The "Madam" must have been what did the trick. There was a murmur about pulling the other one, then the chain clicked and the door opened. I saw that the eagle eye was one of a pair and belonged to a tiny old lady who could have been Petit's mother. By the time we had stepped through, she was pattering back to her own room on carpet slippered feet.

"Make sure you lock up behind you and see to it that dog doesn't do his business. I'm missing Oprah. Nuns from families with bisexual fathers—or something."

Her door closed and there was a rattling of chains and bolts that would have rivaled Marley's Ghost. Maybe Oprah's topic for the day was security around the home.

Anna hadn't even bothered to lock her door and we walked straight in.

Even more than last time, I had the impression of walking on to a very low budget stage set. Everything was there to create an effect. Nothing was there to be lived in.

The bed was stripped, the sheets bunched up by someone in a hurry and left on the floor. The clothes were gone from the rack and an empty

Jack Daniel's bottle lay in the bin among the fragments of broken glasses.

There were only two items of interest in the place.

On the bed lay a blonde wig—chignon style. I doubted the makers would take it back. After all, it was missing at least one hair. I stuffed it in my pocket. I'm a great one for souvenirs.

The other item lay in the corner of the room, where it had obviously been tossed.

It was a canvas picture frame and, when I turned it over, I saw what Holmes had described.

I could recognize Kane's likeness but it was like seeing him through a distorting fairground mirror. The features seemed to be melting, the flesh on the face like running wax. Salvador Dali in manic-depressive mood. The eyes were a fiery red, as if some demon were imprisoned and on the point of breaking free from this loathsome body to be its own even more loathsome self.

The draftsmanship was primitive but the power of the vision was frightening.

Emotion had streamed through the painter's brush straight on to that canvas. But at least it had been in some perverted sense a creative power when the picture was painted. Now someone had turned a negative power on it, for the canvas was scored time and again with slashes and tears. He who creates can destroy. He—or she.

Apartment 13A suddenly seemed an unlucky place to be.

As we let ourselves out, I could hear Oprah addressing the daily faithful. When there was a lull in the ritual applause, I hear Old Eagle Eyes scream out—

"Right on, girl—you tell them cocksuckers!"

Whatever happened to *class*—for Chrissakes!

"So *Anna* Kane killed Mallory?"

We were driving back to my apartment. The rain was heavy now but not torrential and the windscreen wipers were working in fits and starts—mostly fits. I had to pay too much attention to my driving to look at Holmes for his reactions.

"I'm afraid that is for you to determine, Watson. In a sense Anna and Nana Kane were *both* involved. The conflict between them is very real . . ."

"But Nana has won." I made it a statement, though it was really a question.

"Put it this way, my dear chap. I doubt that we shall see Anna Kane again, though I wouldn't bet *all* my army pension on it, if I were you. And you will remember that she said something to the effect that Nicky was 'the only one left,' when you mentioned Mallory. By my admittedly amateur estimation he had been dead for some twenty-four hours by the time we arrived."

"So he was already dead when we were in Anna's apartment?"

There was no answer but then none was necessary. Hands that serve Jack Daniel's also pull triggers.

"There's only one way to settle this once and for all, Holmes. I need to see Nana Kane face to face."

"You also need to catch a certain Bird. Don't lose sight of that, Watson."

"Somehow I think the one will lead me to the other. And Nicky *must* have the Bird. As she said—he's the only one left."

That seemed to satisfy him, for he immediately changed the subject.

"Does that music machine of yours play any *real* music, Watson? A little lively Vivaldi would match my present mood."

As I opened the door of the apartment, I knew right away that something was different. For one thing I didn't remember ordering two extremely large Chinese gentlemen in Italian suits who appeared to be standing waiting for me.

You grow to expect "impassive" from your average Chinese—"imperturbable" even. Call it racial stereotyping, if you will, but there it is. These two took it to another dimension. Their expressions—or, rather, lack of—were carved in stone and hard stone at that. I swear neither of them moved their lips but one of them must have said—

"Mr. Watson. Would you be so kind as to come with us? Our employer wishes to see you."

With an invitation like that and two medium-sized pagodas between you and the drawer in which you keep your trusty Smith & Wesson, one is inclined to go with the flow. And after all, they *had* asked nicely. I indicated I *would* be so kind as to go with them . . .

Somehow they edged me to the door and through it without either of them quite touching me.

"Well, boys, this gives a whole new meaning to Chinese takeaway."

Yes, I know I'd used the line before but *they* hadn't heard it. From their lack of response, they didn't seem to think they'd missed much.

Mike, I felt sure, would savage one or both of them but the older of the two said something to him in Chinese and—can you believe this?—he went into his sit-and-stay routine for the second time. I could only conclude that he must have been a *fu* dog in a previous existence.

Demonstrating a comparable degree of obedience, the stretch limo I'd seen leaving my office earlier rolled to a stop outside the house—just long enough for me to be decanted into the rear half acre and for them to vanish into the mists of the front.

In the half light—the windows were tinted, do I need to mention?—was my old pal, Kai Ling. But there was something different about him. Gone was the white jacket and black trousers and in their place a natty bit of gents' suiting. Savile Row, at a guess. It was more than that, though. His manner was more that of a career diplomat than a cheap hoodlum who went about chopping off people's fingers and turning them into Halloween masks. He might shave off a couple of share points in a business deal or take you to the cleaners in an LBO but that was about it. Shows how little I know.

The man was full of surprises. No sooner had I started to warm the upholstery than I found a flute of champagne in my hand. The condemned man took a hearty snootful. Why not?

"As Bette Davis so aptly put it in *Old Acquaintance.* Warner Brothers. Nineteen Forty-Three—'There comes a time in every woman's life when the only thing that helps is a glass of champagne.' Cheers!" Mr. Cool.

I looked across at Holmes, who was stretching his legs out luxuriously. It was, after all, a pleasant change after the Corvette but he needn't have made it so obvious. He nodded his approval, so I dipped the beak. First Perrier Jouet today. Gallo, eat your heart out.

"Mr. Watson, before this rather tawdry little drama plays itself out, I thought I owed you an apology for some of the *grand guignol* you have been exposed to through the somewhat over-enthusiastic antics of some of my younger associates. They are children, Mr. Watson, over-grown children dedicated to a cause—as, indeed, am I—but lacking the maturity to appreciate the inevitability of gradualness. I believe you have a saying in the West to the effect that everything comes to he—or is it him?—who waits.

"Well, we have waited. Indeed, we have waited. I must admit the Chinese temperament is a boon in this regard. You in the West are anxious to claim credit. Everyone must know that you were the one who did this or achieved that on your watch. We take the longer view. The matter is not personal. Only the desired end is important. That, at least, is our normal pattern but, alas, there are always exceptions and this is one. The sands in the hourglass are fast running out. The Bird's holy millennium is almost upon us and . . . What is that children's game you play? 'Pass the parcel.' It is my destiny to be sitting there when the music stops and, therefore, it is I who am fated to take home the parcel or face the consequences of failure. The latter is not to be contemplated. So, you see, Mr. Watson . . . ?"

He managed to shrug without spilling a drop.

I could see his point of view. I must admit I find it easy to see the point of view of anyone who plies me with vintage champagne.

"So where do I fit into your grand plan?"

"You are, shall we say—'Piggy in the Middle.' Ah, all of this is such good practice for my colloquial English! You have been hired by the loathsome Kane to find the Bird and, although you have so far singularly failed to do so . . ."

That hurt.

". . . you at least seem to have closed certain avenues of exploration. Also you with your pale complexion may move in circles where my colleagues and I would be, perhaps, more noticeable.

"There is one other aspect of this sorry business I should mention and on which we may well have a difference of cultural opinion. It is a tenet of our faith that the infidel must be punished. Anyone who unlawfully possesses the Bird. Over the centuries, from what we can determine, human greed has taken care of that aspect well enough.

"In this present brief episode Mr. Perlman has been taken care of, as has Mr. Mallory. Not by us, as I think you know. The contribution of my associates has been purely cosmetic. Let us attribute it to Fate. The Bird has bitten the hands that fed it, as it always will, and its ways are often devious. There have been others who have given offence and time will take care of them but there is one on whom time may not wait—and that is the person who possesses the Bird at this moment.

"Logic would seem to dictate that that person is Mr. Parmentieri. I come to you with a proposition, Mr. Watson. Help us find the Bird, be our Trojan Horse and we will double anything Mr. Kane has offered you. And after that, we shall be—what is your word?—history. What do you say?"

And then—maybe it was the champagne talking—several things came together in my head that had been bouncing around for the last couple of days. I didn't like any part of this Bird business or the people involved in it—with the possible exception of this strange little Chinese man with his English suit, his French champagne and—I could be fairly sure—his Italian loafers. At least he believed in something. I had an uncomfortable feeling in my inside jacket pocket, where a check was burning a hole. Not because I was dying to deposit it, so that I could see black numbers for a change, but because it didn't belong there. Period. At which point I took it out, tore it up and dropped the pieces on the carpeted floor of the limo. Get the maid to sweep up later!

To cover the psychic shock that act entailed, I helped myself to a refill of P-J. The almond eyes widened a tad, I thought.

"Mr. Chan," I said, "you are looking at a free man. You want your Bird. Well, here's what you do . . ."

For the next several minutes he listened—and

190

so did Holmes—as the limo prowled the streets of Greater L.A.

"It's a little devious," I concluded. He clearly liked devious.

"So you want me to sell drugs to Mr. Parmentieri?"

"No, I want Mr. Parmentieri to think you're going to sell him drugs. Like you, Nicky is between a rock and a hard place. His bosses expect him to deliver and they don't much care how. They're running a business and the drugs let Nicky make his bottom line. It's the good all-American way. Perlman is terminally out of the picture and the connection is blown. Now, I'm betting Mr. P. hasn't quite got round to telling the Pomona family of this unfortunate happenstance and is casting round for alternative sources of supply. He won't feel comfortable with the Colombians. And the last thing he wants is to let old man Kane back into the game. So you, my friend, will look like the answer to a maiden's prayer . . .

"Old English saying," I added in answer to his puzzled expression. "Don't let it bother you."

He thought it over for a while, as we purred on in our tinted time capsule. Then he turned to me with a grin that would have sent a shiver up many a spine.

"So, Mister Plivate Eye, you wish Charlie Chan make likee Dlug Rord, yes?"

191

I cursed bugs and all forms of insect life.

"I'm sorry, Mr. Watson, but I couldn't resist it. Please help me finish the champagne. A toast to our unlikely partnership. There is something highly ironic in even discussing the provision of drugs to a race of people who are steadily gorging themselves to death on a diet of fast food, empty calories and high cholesterol without the need for any further assistance. But if appearing to pander to Western decadence and self-indulgence is the best way to achieve our ends . . . so be it. It could even be considered to be politically correct."

We clinked glasses.

"Now, Mr. Watson, how do you suggest we proceed?"

"Excellent, Watson. I confess I never get your limits. Here have I been thinking that you were being merely buffeted by events, when all the time you were formulating your master plan. My dear fellow, I apologize most humbly."

I waved a modest hand. It would only have undermined that precious confidence for me to tell him that my decision had little to do with the gradual construction of an overarching concept and everything to do with a pigheaded determination not to be used as a psychological football. So now we'd tip all the chips out on the table and let them fall where they may. Frankly, I didn't give a rat's ass *who* had the Bird. A simple search for a spouse of either sex who'd gone walkabout would seem pretty attractive round about now, providing I could keep my noggin intact this time.

But Holmes now had the bit between his teeth.

"I presume, old fellow, you intend to follow the procedure I believe is commonplace in these affairs?"

Procedure. *What* procedure?

"Oh, yes, the usual procedure, certainly."

"Summon all the usual suspects to a single location without giving them reason to suspect the presence of the others and inviting each of them in such a way that they find the invitation irresistible? Capital, old fellow. Capital."

Yes, it was a good idea, wasn't it. I could hardly believe I'd thought of it unaided. I gave Holmes a sharp glance but he didn't quite catch my eye.

"I wonder if I might suggest one small embellishment on this occasion?"

Never let it be said that the pride of the Watsons was too proud to consider an improvement to a master plan.

"I see now the cunning of your asking your friend McNulty to hold back the news of Mallory's death for twenty-four hours and I suggest that a news embargo will prove effective for our purposes.

"Each of the suspects should appear to be invited by the person they most want to meet and their invitations should be spread. In a well-constructed play the author never brings on all his characters at once.

"Miss Grace will think her invitation comes from Mr. Parmentieri, while Kane and Miss Nana will believe they are going to meet Mallory . . ."

"But surely Nana . . ."

"I think you will find that Miss Kane is already into deep denial on that particular subject. Besides, she has her father to contend with and under those circumstances . . .

"Mr. Parmentieri, of course, will be allowed to believe his invitation comes from your new Chinese associate.

"As a venue, may I suggest Mallory's beach house? He is unlikely to require it this evening and it is suitably isolated. I assume you saw the magazine article pinned to the wall of the workroom. He appears to have been very proud of it. The address, unless memory fails me, was Cormorant Cove. We do seem to be infested with birdlife, do we not?"

We were back in my apartment, the limo having dropped us off at the front door.

On the way upstairs we had had a brief exchange with Mr. Gryppe, who had clearly recovered his confidence.

"Some people are flying high, I see." A reference to the departing limo that did, indeed, make the neighborhood look even shabbier by comparison. And maybe he was right. I don't remember being conscious that it touched the ground.

Then, in case that had come out sounding too flattering—

"Haven't heard a peep out of him upstairs. Suppose he's all right." Bang.

Not only was "him upstairs" all right—Mike was still sitting and staying with a beatific expression on his face. It took me all my time to snap him out of it and he was positively grouchy until I'd found some old hamburger at the back of the Frigidaire, which he grudgingly accepted as a *quid pro quo*.

I sank into my favorite chair—for once no one else was competing for it—and put my feet up with a sigh of relief. Frankly, I was no nearer solving the case than I had been when it began but at least I'd played my highest card. Now we'd see what everyone else had in their hand.

It was in the euphoria induced by that conviction and endorsed by Monsieur Perrier (not to mention Jouet) that Holmes had made his surprising remarks.

"Ah, yes, Mallory's beach house. A stormy night. Sea birds calling. Surf pounding. I can see it now. And then the guilty party, wracked by remorse, gives himself—or *her*self . . ." I quickly added, not wishing to appear sexist ". . . away," I ended limply.

"Ah, Watson, it is good to hear that pawky sense of humor of yours at work once more. Frankly, I had wondered over the past day or two whether it had perhaps deserted you but I see not. You, of course, will have primed the psychological pump, so to speak, before any one of them sets foot in the place.

"Now then, old friend, what do you say to our composing the invitations to the party? And incidentally, since we shall need a messenger to deliver them, what harm would there be in our bringing friend Petit into our confidence? He has the added advantage of being able to afford us access to the beach house."

"My thought exactly, Holmes." I crossed everything that would cross. I'm sure I *would* have thought of it—eventually.

I picked up the phone and called Petit.

An hour or so later the three of us were sitting—or, rather, two were sitting and one was hovering—around the card table that served as my desk.

Petit had been pleased and flattered to receive my call and glad of any excuse to leave the gloomy surroundings of Mallory's premises, where he apparently slept on a cot in a back room.

"Everywhere I look I see that silly scarecrow face of his," he said, his own tiny face scrunched

196

up until it resembled nothing so much as one of the gargoyles on Notre Dame. "He was a devious old devil but he was a good friend to me and anything I can do to fix whoever killed him—well, sir, you may count on Dwight G. Grandhomme." He gave me a look which defied me to make something of it.

"My granddaddy was from the South."

Ah, well, that explained it.

By the time he arrived Holmes and I had composed the invitations and I confess I was pleased with them. When I say "Holmes and I," of course, I did the actual writing and, come to think of it, Holmes never said a word. So why did the odd word or phrase drop into my mind unbidden? A thought for another day.

By now Charlie Chan would have made one of his famous "teaser" phone calls to establish contact, so Nicky Parmentieri's note was simple . . .

"My Dear Mr. Parmentieri,

"May I suggest we sample one another's merchandise forthwith, so that our new friendship may be cemented expeditiously? A mutual friend, who is out of town, has made his premises available."

And then the address and time—11:30 p.m. It sounded a little flowery but, hey, what else would a Mafia-educated kid expect from an Oxford-educated Chinaman?

To Kane . . .

"The Bird sings at midnight. There is a golden secret in its song. Be there—or be square. And back to square one. *Sieg heil!*—Q.M."

I was particularly pleased with the rhythm of that one. And the ending would certainly make him sit up in his wheelchair.

To Nana Kane . . .

"If you or your sister ever hope to spread your wings, the Bird will teach you how to fly at midnight tonight—Q.M."

To Linda Grace (I always bet a few bucks on outsiders) . . .

"The situation has changed and we have to make plans right now. My place is too public. Meet me at 11:45 p.m. on the button. N." And then the details.

It was only as I had them all laid out in front of me that I realized something very strange. The handwriting was nothing like my normal scrawl. It had a pleasing calligraphic formality that was almost—Victorian.

A few minutes later Petit—I couldn't handle Grandhomme—had scurried off on his mission and I knew with absolute certainty that nor rain nor snow would prevent the US mails from getting through. Midnight would be a witching hour, one way or another. But who would the wicked witch turn out to be?

Then, to prove that I was still on a roll, I got to

my feet and addressed Holmes, who looked to be on the point of lighting his pipe and putting his feet up. Really—when I'd done all the work!

"Come, Holmes," I cried, "the game's afoot. We haven't a second to lose."

"Where to now, Watson?" And was that a gleam of amusement I detected in those deep-set gray eyes?

"To see the one character we need to complete the cast of our play. We shall pay our respects to Miss Nana Kane . . .

"Mike. Sit and stay!" He grumbled but obeyed. I really *was* on a roll.

THIRTEEN

Kane Towers had an embattled look today. Macbeth could easily have been holed up inside waiting for the fuzz to finger him for the Banquo and Duncan jobs. Never cheerful at the best of times, today it positively loured.

I half expected the chimes to play "Nearer My God To Thee" but it was still Wagner, though in less ebullient mood, I felt.

Today's butler, though, was pure Jeeves. Presumably whoever did the hiring considered a stiffish upper lip was now called for. A solid presence, his face would have graced a coin and his prow a stately man o' war.

"And who shall I say is calling, sir?"

And when I'd told him—"I'm afraid Mr. Kane is not receiving callers today, sir, but *Miss* Kane did lead me to believe that we might expect a visit from you." *Did* she, indeed? "If you will follow me, sir . . ."

I did as requested and found myself in what was presumably the Library. I say "presumably" because, although it was filled with books from floor to ceiling, I would have bet Mike's bottom dog biscuit that none of them had had its spine cracked. They were even arranged in blocks of colored bindings.

Nana Kane was sitting in a wingback chair with her back to the door pretending to read. The butler must have pressed some sort of buzzer, because she knew I was en route and had had time to art direct herself to receive me. Just one small detail wrong. She was either reading an Australian book—or she was holding it upside down.

In a properly-organized world she'd have rung a small hand bell and said—

"I was just about to have tea and cucumber sandwiches. Won't you join me?"

Instead of which, she said—

"I *knew* you'd turn up like a bad penny sooner or later."

She threw the book on a side table. *Also Sprach Zarathustra*. Somehow I hadn't figured her as a reader of Nietzsche. Genetic influence, presumably.

"What do you want?"

If she thought her manner would have me running for the hills, she was sadly mistaken. I wasn't turning my back on anybody or anything until this whole thing was signed, sealed and delivered to—whoever it was signed, sealed and delivered to.

"I just called to return something."

"What can you possibly have of mine?"

"Who said it was *yours?* Actually, it belongs to your sister."

"*Sister?* I don't *have* a sister."

"Maybe you should tell *her* that. She certainly thinks she has one—*you*."

And I pulled the blonde wig out of my pocket and tossed it on to the table.

Nietzsche Meets Blondie . . . Could sell a million, properly marketed.

From the way Nana Kane recoiled, you'd think she was Cleopatra having a sudden change of heart about the desirability of an asp.

"Take that horrible thing away. I hate the sight of it."

"As you wish. Might as well have it complete, though, before we bin it, don't you think?"—

And I reached over and delicately picked a single blonde hair from her sleeve, where it was competing with dark brown silk and ivory lace.

From the corner of my eye I could see Holmes perched in the window embrasure. He applauded silently. "My first glance is always at a woman's sleeve." Lesson learned, Holmes. Thank you.

She pulled her arm away as though my touch had scalded her and stood with her back to me. What she apparently didn't notice, though, was that she was now facing a large mirror in which I could see her reflection.

And what I saw almost unnerved me, for it was as though I were looking at the magic mirror in *Snow White*, where the Queen turns into the wicked witch. Except this time it was the other way around.

Nana turned into Anna before my eyes. The gray eyes lost their somber depths and seemed to positively sparkle by comparison. The chin came up. She even held her body differently, as she turned back to face me.

"Mr. Watson, please forgive my rudeness but I have been under a lot of strain lately, what with my father's health and . . ." She didn't complete the sentence but I could guess what else. Splitting logs is marginally easier than splitting personalities.

"I know you're only here to help us. And as for my "sister," as you call her, I only wish I had a sister sometimes to share the burden. I can only assume there is someone out there who bears a passing resemblance to me. If I run across her, I will most certainly give her this . . ." and she picked up the wig, as if it were a joke between us, and held it up against her face. "After all, it's hardly me, is it?"

"Oh, I don't know, dear. Some people might say it was quite an improvement. Stepmother's little joke, darling. We can take a joke, can't we?"

Standing in the open doorway—and using the frame more for support than decoration—was Linda Grace. She was nursing a highball glass that seemed to have been receiving a lot of recent attention, to judge from the blood red lipstick smears around its rim.

"Well, hello there, Mr. Whatever-Your-Name-Is Private Eye. Missed you at the movies the other day—yesterday, was it?"

This lady wasn't nearly as drunk as she'd like us to believe but the impression was great protective coloring. It may just possibly have been her best part. And it wasn't scripted.

"Didn't miss much. Oh, except the final scene when I fired that fucking fag director . . ."

"Oh," Nana/Anna chimed in sweetly, "is this the film where three old ladies in the twilight home fight it out with zimmer frames?"

"Now, listen, sweetie . . ."

But then she controlled herself and smiled at me from under her lashes, as if to say that we were the only two grown-ups here and I'd understand grown-up talk.

"Listen to her—the original good time that was had by all."

It was a good line, even if I had heard it before.

But Nana was playing *her* scene now. She looked at me. They were competing for the attention of an audience of one.

"You'll find that my stepmother has a movie speech to suit every occasion and, believe me, I've heard them all. They're usually culled from the works of the late, great Bette Davis. It's about now that she says—'Fasten your seat belts. It's going to be a bumpy night.' *All*

About Eve. Twentieth Century-Fox. Nineteen-fifty."

"Fuck you, sweetie!"

"Now, *that* one I can't quite place."

"At least Bette never played boring little—*spinsters!*"

Mistake. Big mistake. Even *I* knew that.

"What about *Now, Voyager*? Warner Brothers. Nineteen—"

Check.

"Yeah, but she turned *into* a glamorous woman."

Mate.

"Will you two overgrown children stop this stupid game at once. It has long outlived its amusement value. Mr. Watson will think we are running an institution for the mentally retarded."

Mr. Watson *knew* they were running at least one called Sunnyvale.

Osgood Kane's silent-running wheelchair now filled the doorway behind them.

It was fascinating to see how Kane's two women reacted.

Nana shook a curtain of dark hair across her face. Linda took a defiant slug of whatever-it-was she was drinking. Both of them shut up.

"And now, Mr. Watson, I presume you are here with news of your assignment? What have you to report?"

"The Bird will be in the hands of its rightful

206

owner by this time tomorrow," I replied. Pretty subtle, huh?

"As of now I am no longer working for you, on account of the fact that I have no stomach for horror comics. And you needn't worry—your check will not be presented. Save it for the Clone Adolf Hitler Fund. Ladies—and I use the word loosely . . . you may go to Hell in your own way. Frankly, my dears, I don't *give* a damn." I'd always wanted to say that line.

And with that, I pushed past them—my exit being only slightly marred by the arrival of the Jeeves lookalike, who took up most of the available door space.

I was pleased to see that several feet in front of his leading waistcoat button he was bearing a silver salver on which reposed three familiar-looking envelopes.

I would have given a great deal to have been a fly on the wall to see their various reactions when they opened them but, unless you're a real home-cured ham, when you've made your exit . . . you've made your exit. No "Take Two" in the Theatre, laddie.

Well, they won't have Richard Nixon—or even Jack Watson—to push around any more, I thought. Come to think of it, that's not such a great analogy. I'm glad I only *thought* it.

"Masterly, Watson," said Holmes as he drifted by my side on the long trek to the front door and freedom. "That should give them something to think about until we meet at Philippi."

"Cormorant Cove, surely, Holmes?"

"One and the same, old fellow. One and the same."

FOURTEEN

You had to hand it to Quentin Mallory. He had the Gothic touch. He had christened his beach house Ghormenghast after the Mervyn Peake novel and the fact that .001% of his visitors ever got the point was precisely the point.

It nestled—or perhaps clung would be a better word—to a promontory of bleak rock on a piece of shoreline north of L.A. that was deservedly unfashionable. Despite rising land values, nobody else had built anywhere near it. Most of the trees around it were dead or dying and the cruel sea snapped at its skirts. Was it my imagination or were those Charles Addams bats flitting around us?

I parked the Corvette in some dense shrubbery behind the house, where it couldn't be seen by anyone approaching the place on supposedly legitimate business. Mike made a move to join us but Daddy was firm.

"Stay and guard. *Stay*! Good boy!"

We were making real progress with this "Stay!" business. Maybe it was the slight Chinese inflection I had introduced. It produced a slight curl to the lip—his not mine—but he stayed.

Holmes and I moved purposefully, I hoped, towards Ghormenghast . . .

As we approached, a door yawned open and standing there, like a baby's first tooth, stood Petit. He moved aside to let me enter, then closed the door behind us both.

"I've done as you asked, Mr. Watson," he said, oddly formal. "All the inside doors are locked and bolted, except the main living room that looks out over the ocean. That's the only room anyone can get into. I've left the front door obviously ajar. Will there be anything else?"

"No, thank you, Mr. Grandhomme." I returned the formality. "I suggest you return to your own room and lock yourself in. What happens from now on need not concern you. I shall try to see to it that the right thing happens. And I am most grateful to you."

We exchanged courtly bows and he disappeared into the recesses of the house. A few moments later I heard the key turn in a lock.

"You know, Watson," said Holmes, "I always thought that, if I had not decided to track down the criminal element in our society, I might have made an excellent burglar. I'm sure I should have risen to the top. And with my present advantages . . . But then, where would have been the amusement in that?

"Still, we had our moments, did we not, old fellow—entering premises with burglarious intent, when the normal channels were closed to us? Ah, the game, Watson, the game!"

And with that, he drifted off to examine the setting of our little drama.

Through the floor to ceiling windows that opened on to the ocean it was clear that Mother Nature had been recruited to create an appropriate setting. The storm front that had been hovering around the area had now decided to pay a return visit. Ominous black clouds were playing tag with the moon and the man on timpani was tuning up somewhere in the hills behind us, while in the distance lightning was saying something in semaphore. All in all, Hitchcock would have been hard put to find a better setting for a *dénouement*.

Now, how best to set the scene? The room was large and open in its layout with a casual arrangement of sofas and easy chairs. A grand piano stood near the windows that took up the whole of the main exterior wall. I could just imagine Mallory sitting there playing Wagner loudly to a chorus of seabirds, while the white muslin curtains danced, Gatsby-like in the breeze that gently ruffled his designer hair.

All very charming but where were the heavy velvet drapes the private eye is supposed to hide behind, while the guilty party confesses all? Nowhere to be seen, that's where. Under the piano? I think not. Too undignified to extricate oneself at the *moment critique*. It somehow didn't fit in with my image of Marlowe to see him hopping around with cramp while struggling with the Bad Guy.

Seeing me look around hopelessly, Holmes came up with the solution.

"As I'm sure you noticed, old fellow, these are French windows that open outwards. I feel sure the mechanism can be so ordered that one of them will not close properly. This will enable you to take cover in the oleander bushes I noticed on the terrace outside. From that point of vantage you will be able to hear what transpires in the room itself and make your entrance in timely fashion."

Well, of course, that would have occurred to me momentarily but I was grateful for Holmes's intervention, for even now I could hear the sound of a car approaching and see the glare of its headlights, as it turned off the highway on to the promontory that defined Cormorant Cove. I consulted my tired old Timex. 11:30 on the nose. If my plan was working, it should be Nicky Parmentieri and, indeed, the macho roar of the exhaust pre-empted the arrival of an open top Beemer. Just the sort of overt statement I would have expected from him. But then, I was more than a little jealous, if the truth be known.

The reflection from the headlights flashed briefly across the window, as he turned the corner of the house into the parking lot. Once the car was safely out of sight, I slipped out of the window and took up my position in the bushes Holmes had indicated. From there, as he had predicted, I had a clear view of the whole room and in two steps I could be inside. Holmes, I noticed, had taken up a position behind the piano. He nodded in my direction to indicate that I could not be seen. The stage was set. All we needed now were our actors.

We didn't have long to wait.

Nicky Parmentieri came round the door as carefully as a paintbrush applying a final coat. Though, come to think of it, I couldn't remember seeing a paintbrush carrying a gun before. He moved round the room, keeping his back always to the wall, until he'd checked out every inch of it. I was watching a man who'd done this a time or two before.

Finally, he settled by the piano and took in the view, which by now was truly spectacular. Sheet lightning was moving steadily in from the ocean and, every time Nature's house lights blinked on and off, I could see battalions of white-capped waves marching like Storm Troopers towards the shore below us. It was an effect Wagner would have killed for and it would surely have inspired him to come up with a stirring little dirge. Somehow—this being Hollywood and all—it seemed eminently appropriate for our very own *film noir*.

Nicky reached into his pocket for something that was badly distorting its immaculate line. The object appeared reluctant and it caused him to put his gun down on the piano lid, so that he could use both hands.

Finally, he pulled a package some four inches square wrapped in gray chamois leather. He placed it carefully on the piano and unwrapped it as though it was the Shroud of Turin. Which, in a sense, it was. For there, gleaming against the gray of the leather and the polished black of the piano was the Borgia Bird.

As if on cue, there was the brightest flash of lightning yet and I could have sworn the Bird's eyes blazed with anger. The timing was so dramatic that it caused Nicky to step back involuntarily. Then, realizing what he'd done, he caught himself and smiled a foolish little smile. Good job the Family hadn't seen their star pupil frightened by a little lightning.

It must have been the brightness of the lightning that prevented any of us from seeing the headlights of the next car to arrive. The occupant was in the house and moving towards the door of the living room before Nicky heard them. Quickly, he re-wrapped the Bird and then posed himself nonchalantly against the piano. Anyone entering the room would see him against the dramatic backdrop. A powerful man with the power of Nature at his command. Very Otto Kruger or Dan Duryea.

"Come in, Mr. Chan, I was expecting you."

Oh, that Kai Ling (or whatever). What a sense of humor!

Nicky had probably never *heard* of Charlie Chan.

"Well, I've been called a few things in my time but never Mr. Chan. Are you sure you've got the right house, darling. Or are you auditioning for something?"

And Linda Grace made her entrance. And "entrance" was the only word for it. Where Nicky had slunk, she sashayed. I hadn't seen it done that well since Mae West but there was something vaguely pathetic about it, nonetheless. This was an assertive action to boost her own confidence in herself.

Nicky's "What the hell are you doing here?" can't have done much to aid the process.

Her eyes widened at his tone but she pressed on, as though she hadn't noticed.

"What is this, darling, premature Alzheimer's? You *asked* me to meet you here. Remember? You said that the situation had changed and that we had to make our plans right away. So here I am. When do we leave, Nicky? I can't wait to get away from Hell House and that decaying old vulture. Where are we going to—Rio? Tahiti? Anywhere. I don't care. My fans will miss me, of course, but God knows I gave them my all for all those years. To hell with them. It's *our* time now, babe—just you and me . . ."

And then she tried the move that had never failed her yet. She rubbed herself up against Nicky and leaned up with eyes closed to be kissed.

There are few sights sadder than a beautiful woman—and make no mistake, Linda Grace was still a beautiful woman—waiting to be kissed and then not *being* kissed. It took her several beats before she realized there was nothing doing and another few before she could accept it.

Slowly her eyes opened and she took a step back. But then the look of a dead lizard in Nicky's eyes would have caused anyone to think twice.

"What's the matter, Nicky? Why are you looking at me like that? It's something bad, isn't it?"

Nicky put his hands on her shoulders, as you would when trying to talk sense into a wayward child.

"Look, Linda, I *wasn't* expecting you and I was going to tell you this later but maybe now is as good a time as any. Things *have* changed—changed for the better, as far as I'm concerned. I've got a really big deal going through that will tie things up nicely and get me outta here. I've got a buyer for the goddam Bird . . ."

He turned from her and picked up the package from the piano. Once again he unwrapped it as carefully as if it had been his first born and, once again, the Bird flamed in that dimly-lit room. And—I know it sounds corny as hell—but I swear the lightning flashed on cue, making the Bird seem to blink at its surroundings.

"The only thing they don't know is that the Bird I'm going to hand over will be a copy I've had made—not this little beauty."

And he stroked its golden head. For a moment I thought he was about to kiss it.

"So I get the deal and I get to keep the Bird. And any time I want my fuck-you money, I've got it right here. As good as Fort Knox and a lot less trouble."

That, I thought, was a debatable subject for another time and place. So Mallory had been a prodigal intermediary indeed. Replicas Anonymous. Somehow I thought Nicky was underestimating the sagacity of our mutual oriental buddy—not to mention his scalpel-happy associate. But that was *his* problem.

He soon found himself with another.

"So you see, kid, it's a chance of a lifetime. I got to take it."

He gave her the crooked boyish grin that probably worked just about as regularly as Linda's physicality but this time his audience wasn't buying the show.

"In a minute you'll be telling me that where you're going I can't follow, what you've got to do, I can't be any part of and that I have to understand that the problems of two little people don't amount to a hill of beans in this crazy world. Well, Nicky, my love, I'm not buying into this *Casablanca* crap. We're in this together. I've put everything on the line for you, you arrogant little *schmuck*!"

"Now, c'mon, kid . . . We've had some good times, a few laughs. Nobody said it was forever."

"And don't call me kid! You're no Bogie."

I somehow doubted patience was Nicky's strong suit. Now the spoiled child came out and at the same time you could see in the set of his face the mean man he would age into. The mouth tightened and there was nobody home behind the eyes.

"Yeah, I guess you're right, Linda. I really shouldn't call you, kid, should I? You haven't been a kid for many a long day. How *many* days, Linda? Hundreds?

"Thousands? Let's take a look, shall we?"

Suddenly he grabbed her by the hair and wound his hand deep in it. With the other he seized her upper arm so hard that she gasped. Then he turned her around so that they could see themselves reflected as a couple in a large Venetian mirror close to the piano.

The glass had that hazy texture, so that they seemed to be floating to the surface of a lake.

"Take a look, Linda. Take a *good look!* I'm

thirty. You're what? Fifty? And I'm being kind. Why would I settle for Second-hand Rose when I can have the pick of the crop?"

And he pushed her in front of him, so that she was almost touching the mirror. The table light on the piano flared up at her face, cruelly exposing the powder-caked lines around her eyes, the grooves on each side of the mouth where her lip gloss cunningly continued where the natural lip line left off. It was a moment when all the perfumes of Arabia and all the skills of Elizabeth Arden wouldn't save a woman from facing Old Mother Time.

I could read the shock in her eyes. She'd never let herself see this kind of truth. As I've said before and I'll say again, Linda Grace was a truly beautiful woman but Time was slowly calling in its IOUs. And woe betide the man who brings a woman to that realization.

Nicky Parmentieri was too young and thoughtless to realize that. He was also too insensitive to see that the woman who turned away from the mirror when he released her was a different one from the one he had made to face it.

Now *Linda's* was the empty face, while Nicky was becoming angry and excited.

"Listen, baby, you were great—the best. But you've had your moment. Mine's ahead of me. When the deal's through, I'll see you right, I promise. You name it. But this is it. *Sayonara.*

219

End of the road. Get it? What do you say?"

And then a mouse with icy feet ran up the small of my back as I saw Linda's eyes. I'd seen that wide open expression only once before, where the whites are visible right around the pupils. That was Gloria Swanson as Norma Desmond in *Sunset Boulevard*, when she comes down the staircase and says—"I'm ready for my close-up, Mr. De Mille." And, to tell you the truth, I'd thought she was simply an old silent star over-acting. But Linda Grace was now *living* that part—or one very like it.

"Oh, Jerry," she said, moving slowly around Nicky and never taking those stare-y eyes from his face. Nor could he seem to shift his gaze. She was mesmerizing him.

"Don't let's ask for the moon. We have the stars."

"What are you talking about? Who the hell is 'Jerry'?"

But *I* knew. Linda Grace had retreated to the security of the movies, where life was lived as it was supposed to be lived and you knew what you had to do and how it would all turn out. Jerry was the Paul Henreid character who played opposite Bette Davis in *Now, Voyager*, where the plain Jane gets the gorgeous guy.

But now she was into something else . . .

"Nothing can harm us now. What we have can't be destroyed. That's our victory—our victory over the dark. It's a victory because we're not afraid."

Bette Davis again. *Dark Victory* this time. Those hours in the cheap seats hadn't been wasted after all. But where was she going with this?

Somebody who was now distinctly afraid was Nicky Parmentieri. I could see the perspiration on his forehead even from where I stood and this was not a humid night. Linda kept circling him and as she did so, he kept turning to face her. It was the mongoose and the snake and I had no idea which was which.

"OK, Linda, you've had your fun. Cut out all that movie crap and get real. We've both got our lives to get on with."

"But the movies *are* real, darling. It's the rest that's shit. And talking of lives—you've just *had* yours. Nobody *leaves* Linda Grace. *I'm* the one who leaves. Goodbye, Nicky!"

There was the sound of a shot, then another. If a director had asked Nicky to register amazement, he could never have done it half as well as he did at that moment. The eyes widened even more than Linda's, the mouth opened and he turned to clutch at the piano.

It was only then I realized that in her movements around Nicky and her persistent eye contact Linda had managed to scoop up his gun from the piano without his noticing.

Blind instinct now drove him to reach for what was no longer there. His hand scrabbled pointlessly over the polished surface and encountered only the Borgia Bird in its wrapping. As he fumbled at it, the chamois fell away and he had the golden object in his hand for a fleeting moment before Linda began firing again, this time into his unprotected back.

Nicky fell at her feet—not in the gradual, balletic fashion of a movie death but ludicrously and all at once, like a marionette when the puppet master has removed his hand.

Linda emptied the magazine into him, then stood staring down at him.

Then she looked up and for an instant I thought she could see me but it was the lens of a movie camera in her mind that had her full attention.

"With all my heart, I still love the man I killed."

Davis couldn't have delivered the line better—even though she had delivered it *first* in *The Letter.*

The storm chose that moment to deliver its first clap of thunder. It was virtually overhead and for a moment it deafened me. Then it began to roll around the neighboring hills, like busybody neighbors passing on gossip.

"Bravo!"

The voice was both ironic and metallic.

The doorway was now filled by Kane's wheelchair. In it he sat, tapping his wizened arm on the metal armrest, as if in applause. Behind him, still in the shadows, stood the figure of Nana. How long had they been there? How much had they seen?

"Poor little Nicky. You wouldn't listen to any of us, would you? Well, this is what happens when you play out of your league."

He turned to address his daughter.

"Nana, my dear, I believe Mr. Parmentieri has something that belongs to me. I believe he placed it on the piano when he began the scene with my about-to-be-ex-wife. Would you be so good as to bring it to me?"

Something in his voice brought Linda back from wherever she had been. She turned her face in his direction and it was like that moment in *She* when time and nature suddenly catch up with Ayesha, She-Who-Must-Be-Obeyed. Linda Grace had aged ten years in as many minutes. It was the face of an old woman that tried to focus on Kane.

Then instinct seemed to take over. She snatched up the Bird and held it to her like a precious baby.

"Oh, but you can't have this. Nicky and I need it. It's our meal ticket. You see, we're going away together, me and Nicky. Going to start over in _____. I can't remember where. Where is it, Nicky? Where are we going to start over . . . ?"

That was when Nana shot her.

A small gun had somehow appeared in her hand as she crossed the room and it didn't take much detecting to guess that this was the .22 that had killed Mallory.

They say that a .22 is unreliable at anything but close range but then, Nana Kane had been practising lately. Her shot was right on the money—in more ways than one. It took Linda right in the heart and a small red carnation began to blossom in her cleavage, until it turned into a full, then over-blown rose and she sank slowly and elegantly to the floor. It was almost certainly the best death scene the lady had ever played.

Nana walked over to the body and bent down. She bent down as Nana Kane but when she stood up again and turned towards her father, she had the face of Anna. She also had in the palm of her hand the remains of the Borgia Bird. The shot that took out Linda Grace had taken the Bird with it.

"Oh, Daddy,"—it was the voice of a little frightened girl—"I couldn't help it. The nasty lady wouldn't give it to me, so I had to do it. I didn't mean to hurt the birdie. Really, I didn't."

She went over to him with tentative steps and laid what was left of the Bird in his lap. Then she stood back, as if a little distance would protect her from the heat of his anger.

I looked at Kane's face. But where I had expected to see malice and fury there was only sadness and defeat. He held the fragment up and, once again, it was as though the creature was a lightning conductor.

The storm was now right above us and the thunder and lightning were simultaneous this time. The flash showed for a brief instant what Kane had seen. The Bird was hollow, the thin metal casing packed with stone or cement to give it the required weight.

With surprising strength, a strength born of frustration, Kane hurled it from him. It seemed to travel in an arc in slow motion and my eyes followed it until it reached the mottled Venetian mirror in which the images of Nicky and Linda were reflected. Their bodies seemed almost posed in a Romeo and Juliet tableau of death, until with a crash, the image shattered, like a stone disturbing the surface of a pond.

Now the crazy paving image showed Nana. Gone was the frightened Anna. This was the vengeful Nana standing over the bodies and venting on them the varied gutter vocabulary I had heard that night in Birdland. The expression on that twisted face scared me almost more than anything I had seen so far. And what scared me even more was when she loosed off another two shots into the bodies of Linda and Nicky. Isn't there some rule about not shooting a man—let alone a lady—when she's down? If not, there should be.

It was time to call a halt. There was nothing more to be gained here. Two people were dead and there *was* no bird. Perhaps there never had been. Perhaps it was all for nothing.

I pulled open the French window and stepped into the room. Holmes materialized at my side.

"Party's over, kiddies."

All the time I had been in the shrubbery I had had Mr. Smith and Mr. Wesson by my side, cocked and ready to roll. Now I used them to cover Nana.

"Drop the gun on the floor, Miss Kane." Nothing like a little formality to remind people we live in a civilized society—occasionally. "Nice and easy on the floor there."

She turned—and Anna said:

"Oh, hi, Jack, where did you come from? You really should have been here sooner. You could have helped me. I told you about the terrible things Nana's been doing. She was fucking Nicky until that bitch Linda came along with her painted eyes and her big boobs. And Nicky was so sweet. And then she stole Daddy's precious Bird and gave it to that creep Perlman to give to Nicky. But then I don't know what happened. The Bird got lost somehow. We thought Mr. Mallory might have it but he didn't and he was awfully nasty about it, so she had to kill him. So Nicky *had* to have it, don't you see? But he didn't have it, either. So what can you do,

Jack? Birdie fly away . . . Birdie go bye-bye."

Then she laughed the piercing, spine-chilling laugh of a demented child.

And then she shot *me*.

I guess all the words and the flickering expressions crossing her lovely face had mesmerized me, as they were intended to. Anna-Nana-Anna. Now you see her, now you don't. But Nana had won in the end.

The bullet took me in the right shoulder and I've been shot often enough to know the routine.

You know you've been hit but the body's immediate reaction is to numb the place, so you don't feel a thing. It's later that it begins to hurt like hell—if you're lucky. If you're not, then you *still* don't feel a thing. Ever.

I tried to raise my own gun but Mr. Smith and Mr. Wesson seemed to have put on weight. I did just manage to pull the trigger. Nothing. The damn thing had jammed.

Then I found myself on the floor, slumped against the open window. Nana was walking towards me with that loony smile on her face and that cute little gun in her hand. She'd have a busy day tomorrow carving all those new notches on it. Pity I wouldn't be around to see which one was mine.

Now her image was beginning to come and go, in and out of focus. I told myself—Marlowe wouldn't faint at a time like this. Sam Spade wouldn't pass out. Hang in there, Watson! At least go out cracking wise. But I couldn't think of a single funny thing to say. Life itself was one big joke but it would take too long to explain that to a mad lady.

Then I saw Holmes do the strangest thing. He put his lips together and seemed to be whistling. Funny thing to do at a time like this, Holmes, I felt like saying. I hope it's your favorite Wagner. Let me go out like a Valkyrie. That's right. Jack Watson, Last of the Valkyries.

I saw Nana raise the gun until I was looking down the long thin tunnel of its barrel. So T. S. Eliot was wrong. The world *did* end with a bang. I just hoped I wouldn't whimper.

Suddenly in my dimming peripheral vision I sensed a blur of movement. Something had passed my shoulder and was now attached to Nana Kane's arm. It was also making familiar growling noises and she was screaming in the key of—was it C? For some reason she also seemed to have dropped her gun at my feet. I picked it up with my left hand and levered myself upright by leaning on the window frame.

Nana Kane seemed to have acquired Mike. Or perhaps Mike had acquired Nana Kane. As he hung there, those great limpid eyes—Mike's not Nana's—found mine, as if to say—"OK, boss, what do I do now?"

I told him he had probably better let go. After all, I did know where she'd been.

Mike dropped to the floor and padded over to sit at my feet. Ah, those dog training classes are worth every penny. Mike's going to one as soon as I can afford it.

"Thank you, Holmes," I muttered. I didn't care if anyone else heard but no one did. Nana was rocking to and fro, nursing her arm and whimpering like the overgrown, if lethal, schoolgirl she really was. Linda and Nicky seemed to have no comment. And Kane . . . ?

Kane was sitting in his chair, as always, but now slumped to one side. Since I'd known him it had never been what you might call a pretty face but now it was as though gravity had pulled one side of it down. He was still breathing—just about—but he had had a massive stroke. Only the eyes were alive but the being that was Osgood Kane was trapped for whatever time he had left in this sad sack of skin and bone as surely as if he had been buried in an underground prison with— what was Wilde's famous description? "That patch of blue that prisoners call the sky."

The phone was by the piano and I risked putting Nana's gun down long enough to dial left handed. Nobody here was going no place. At least, no place of their own choosing.

McNulty picked up his cell phone on the first ring.

"A delivery for you, you Irish Mick," I said. Then it seemed a good time to faint.

That bottomless black pool had never looked so inviting. As I sank, I could swear I heard Holmes's voice say anxiously—

"You're not hurt, Watson. For God's sake, say that you are not hurt!"

And somehow it seemed to me that he had said that to me somewhere before but, then, how could he? Still, it pleased me strangely.

FIFTEEN

Michelle Pfeiffer was leaning over to kiss me.

"Looks like he's waking up," she said softly.

The only trouble was, as her lovely face came slowly into focus, it turned into the homely mug of McNulty. Rats!

Hovering over his shoulder was Holmes and, from what I could make out, the rest of the room was awash with paramedics. From where I lay, propped up on one of the sofas, I could see two black body bags being carried out on stretchers. Linda and Nicky—united in death, at least. So Linda had kept her man, though she'd undoubtedly have preferred a less passive union.

"At a guess I'd say this place looks like the last scene of one of those Elizabethan tragedies. Only isn't *everybody* supposed to be dead?"

"McNulty, that mordant sense of humor of yours will be the death of me. If it hadn't been for the dog in the night time, I wouldn't presently be among those present myself."

I felt a wet tongue lick my face and it most certainly wasn't Michelle Pfeiffer's. Nor, fortunately, was it McNulty's. Mike was sitting by the side of the sofa and hearing my voice had brought on this bout of spontaneous affection. I reached out with my uninjured hand and scratched his ears.

"Thanks, pal. I owe you one."

"I'll say you do. You owe me several."

McNulty obviously wasn't a dog owner. He assumed I was talking to him.

"The doc's patched you up for now. He says you're lucky it was only a rinky-dink little bullet and it missed anything important—supposing you *had* anything important. You'll be as good as new in a couple of days—not that that's saying a lot. Now, how about telling your Uncle Mac just what went down here tonight before the US Cavalry got here?"

So I did—most of it. I left out the China Connection. Somehow conspiring to deal in drugs, even nonexistent ones, wouldn't look too good on my report card. But *crime passionelle*, now that sounds really sexy.

"So Nicky's out of the game?" he said when I'd finished. "The Pomonas will probably send in some other goon to replace him—but then again, maybe they'll think it's more trouble than it's worth. After all, we're a long way from St. Louis. We can but live in hopes. Pity about Linda Grace, though. I used to fantasize about her when I wasn't worrying about my acne. . . . God, that was how many years ago?" He paused for a moment's thought. "Guess that was part of her problem. Right?"

I sat up, so that I could see the rest of the room better. The pain wasn't too bad at all and I guessed I'd been given a jab of something or other.

Outside the window Nature seemed to have decided that it had given us its best shot with the storm and all—or maybe it felt it couldn't compete with the theatrics going on indoors. In any case, it had shut up shop for the night and now—would you believe it?—a full moon was trying to con us that it had been there all the time.

As I turned towards the doorway, Nana Kane came towards me, flanked on each side—I was relieved to see—by two policewomen. She'd been cuffed but had managed to raise both hands so that she could suck her thumb.

"We found her like that when we got here. Haven't been able to get a peep out of her. The only time she's taken her goddam thumb out of her goddam mouth was when we cuffed her and then it went right back in again. Personally, I think she's out to lunch and I wouldn't count on her being back for tea."

When she was opposite me, she turned her head in my direction.

McNulty was right. The eyes were empty caverns measureless to man. Deep in their recesses Nana was probably arguing with Anna and who knew how many other schizoid siblings but they could keep the outcome to themselves, as far as I was concerned. I dropped my own eyes and the parade passed by.

"What about the old man?"

"Doc says it's a stroke and they've taken him to the hospital. But he's a tough old buzzard, that one. He's not ready to call it a day yet and there's nothing much they can do for him. My guess is they'll send him home and wait for Father Time to take care of things. He's got more nurses there than the Good Samaritan anyway and there's not a damn thing we can charge him with."

I reflected that Osgood Kane—Otto Kreizer—or whatever his name was had been living in his personal hell for many a year now. He'd just moved down one layer. But the thought seemed too existential to bother McNulty with at the moment.

"Well, I think that about wraps it up for now, Watson, *mon vieux*. We'd better get you home. You can come in and make a statement when you're felling up to it. None of these squirrels is going anywhere. I'll get one of my guys to drive that heap of junk you call a car. You really should invest in a new one—you make my crime scenes look shabby . . ."

I thought of the torn scraps of Kane's check that had been earmarked for just that purpose. Ah, well . . .

"Come on, pooch. Sounds like you earned your keep tonight."

And McNulty reached over to scratch Mike's ears, too. Twice in one day. And they say dogs don't grin. Ear to ear *and* a thump from that apology for a tail.

Home, James . . .

"I beg you not to exert yourself, Watson. With your medical training you of all people should know that rest is of the essence. I would offer to help but under my present circumstances . . ."

Holmes, Mike and I were back in the apartment and, due to my invalid status, I had been given the choice of chair. I had also been allowed the last beer in the house, even though the qualified competition for it was not significant and I had had to fetch it myself. Hence Holmes's strictures.

"Holmes," I said, not quite catching his eye. "I want to thank you for what you did back there. But for you, I'd be a crime statistic by now."

"My dear old fellow,"—and I thought I heard a small catch in *his* voice, too—"how often have you not done something of the sort for me in other days?"

Then, so as to change a potentially embarrassing subject for both of us, he went on—"Of course, had you taken your old service revolver, as I suggested, instead of that piece of glorified tin, a lot of effort could have been saved. However . . .

"I suggest we now review the events of the last few days, for I am sure you will want to add this little affair to your other chronicles in due course."

I was too tired to understand what he was referring to but I let it pass.

So we did as he suggested and then I came to the question that was still bugging me.

"So there never was a Borgia Bird—a real one, I mean? All that killing was for nothing?"

"Oh, most certainly there was a Bird but it was the idea of the Bird that led to the carnage—as it always has. It was enough for each of them to *think* they possessed it."

"But where is it now?"

"We'll come to that in good time, old fellow." He would tell me when he was ready and nothing would hurry him.

"The saddest aspect of the whole affair is undoubtedly the daughter. Kane himself, of course, is as close to pure evil as one will ever see. He reminds me of earlier adversaries of ours—Grimesby Roylott and Charles Augustus Milverton are two who come to mind. You may wish to refresh your memory of those cases before you take up your pen on this one.

"So Nana Kane may well have inherited those tainted genes but that does not necessarily doom the offspring. What undoubtedly did was the conditioning she received at her father's hand. Good and evil clearly fought an ongoing battle in her developing mind until the tension became too great to bear and she created sister Anna as an *alter ego*.

"Young Sigmund Freud was doing some fascinating work in this area of—'schizophrenia,' I believe he called it at the end of my time in practice. He would have relished this case. I don't know if you ever met him, Watson? Ah well, it is of no matter.

"Alas, the dark power was the stronger, as it so often is, and from that point the outcome was inevitable. But try and remember *Anna* Kane, Watson. In her own way she was every bit as real as Nana and she clearly felt some affinity for you, felt that you might be able to help her. And had things been otherwise—who knows? But seeing her lover lost to her . . ."

We sat in silence for a few moments and I noticed the first tentative fingers of dawn toying with the venetian blind.

"But the Bird, Holmes. Where is the Bird?"

"Where it has been all along, my dear fellow. And where you will discover it when you have had some sleep. No . . ." he raised his hand in protest, as I started to get up—"on this occasion *I* am *your* medical advisor. And besides, it is not going to fly away, I promise you."

And with that, he folded his hands in front of him, leaned back in his chair and closed his eyes. I could tell from a contented whiffling sound that Mike was already in doggie dreamland, no doubt fantasizing about which other human body parts he could append himself to, Dog-on-the-Arm having been such a palpable hit. Come to think of it, I was feeling more than a little sleepy mys . . .

SIXTEEN

I must have slept through the phone, for when I came to, the red message light was blinking like the flasher on a blue and white. All that was missing was the siren.

I immediately thought "McNulty" but McNulty could never aspire to those modulated tones.

"My dear Mr. Watson, I am merely calling to inquire after your wellbeing. It was as much as I could do to prevent my more proactive colleagues from joining in the general mayhem. But once it became clear that the Bird had flown, shall we say, there seemed little point. You did your best, my dear sir, and for that I am truly grateful.

"As you Americans say—rather pointlessly, I might add—'You win a few, you lose a few.' A sentiment worthy of a fortune cookie—or even the blessed Confucius. Oh, and what is that other saying—'The beat goes on'?"

The second call *was* McNulty.

"Funny thing. Our pal Nicky was being bugged. Neat little number under his lapel. Know anything about it?"

Know anything about it? Did fortune cookies have mottoes? Did chopsticks come in pairs?

Then the dial tone took over.

"A patient people, the Chinese. I hardly think

239

we need concern ourselves on Mr. Chan's behalf. And now, Watson, if you are ready. You can, as you are fond of saying, grab a cup of coffee on the way."

"The way to where?"

"The emporium of Quentin Mallory, of course . . ."

My shoulder was stiff but I could manage to drive. I thought of it as a war wound. Would it play up in wet weather, so that I could grimace bravely and win the sympathetic attention of lovely women? I somehow doubted it.

Mallory's showroom had the deserted look of a film set that is about to be dismantled and taken to the back lot for storage until someone wanted to remake one of those Universal house of horror movies.

The impression was only heightened when the door swung open as soon as I pulled up and there was Igor—I mean Petit—standing in the doorway. He rushed over to help me out of the Corvette and was positively solicitous.

"Oh, Mr. Watson, thank heaven you're still with us. I'm not very brave and when the shooting started, I'm afraid I ran. Then I told myself— 'Mr. Watson is doing this to help your old friend.' So I went back and helped the police clear up. You did a fine thing, sir, and on behalf of the late Mr. Mallory and myself, I thank you."

He gave his formal little bow and held out

his hand. I shook it awkwardly with my left. Then we *both* bowed. Nothing like old world courtesy.

"I know why you're here. You think the Bird must be here and you may well be right. But I've looked everywhere all over again since I got back and I know every inch of this place.

"Mallory was affected by it, just like everyone else. We made these copies of it—several of them. Some were only intended as approximate replicas and nobody could have been fooled by those. But as he got into it, he had me make a few that were so close to look at that I flatter myself they would have deceived anyone but the original artist.

"One was for Kane, of course, his *doppelganger* Bird, so to speak. The other Mr. Mallory wanted for himself. I could hear him talking to it, when he thought he was alone. I thought it was sort of a consolation prize after he had to return the original to Kane. But now I'm thinking maybe the clever old devil never did return the original. Maybe he kept it like Kane and gloated over it in secret. Nobody could see it but him and nobody knew he had it. I've heard of collectors who do that."

Holmes's voice was close to my ear.

"Suggest he looks through the showroom again and you'll look in the workshop."

That seemed to make sense to Petit and off

241

he went. A moment later I could hear him rummaging around in the next room.

"What now, Holmes?"

"As I told you, old fellow, I cannot *solve* the problem for you. I can merely point you in a certain direction. There is a nice irony here, for the solution is one that nearly eluded me in one of my past cases. You will remember it as 'The Musgrave Ritual' . . ."

"The one where you found the burial site of the ancient crown of England?"

"Excellent, Watson. Just so. The old manuscript that contained the doggerel verse gave precise measurements leading to the treasure which I followed carefully—and found myself at a dead end. Hold on to that fact.

"Now—do you recall that when Mallory was talking about himself that day, he made a rather obscure reference . . . think, old fellow, think!"

I could see that elegant, elongated figure as he teased Petit. Now, what was it he'd said? I remember it had seemed the affected imagery of an old queen.

Suddenly it came to me.

"He said something about being 'Caesar's wife.' No, he said that, when it came to secrets, he was the *opposite* of Caesar's wife."

"And Caesar's wife was . . . ?" Holmes prompted.

" 'Above reproach.' "

"Which means . . . ?"

"Mallory was *beneath!*"

"Capital, old fellow!"

"And in the Musgrave Ritual, I remember now. You had followed all the instructions, except for the three last words, which didn't seem to mean anything. 'And then under.' The treasure was at the point you had reached but under your feet.

"So the Bird is beneath—but beneath *what?*"

"What was Mallory's actual phrase?"

I racked my brain again and then I heard Mallory say—"I think I'm safe in saying that." His *safe,* of course. But his safe had been ransacked and there was clearly nothing there. What else was it he'd said? "Surface impressions can be deceptive."

Then all the pieces fell into place and I saw where Holmes had been leading me. From somewhere I suddenly had total recall of the Musgrave case, almost as if I *had* written the account myself.

"And then under" had been the three words that unlocked that secret—just as "beneath" was the key to this one.

Mallory had hidden the Bird *underneath* his safe! Where do you hide a leaf? In the forest. Where do you hide something precious when your safe isn't safe? In the last place anyone would think of looking, because lightning isn't supposed to strike in the same place twice. Oh, no?

"Mr. Grandhomme," I called out, "I wonder if I could enlist your services for a moment?"

I heard the sound of small feet scurrying as I moved over to the safe. Holmes was already there when I reached it, smiling like a teacher whose backward pupil had finally got the hang of quadratic equations. It stood in a corner with its mouth hanging open and its contents of papers regurgitated on the floor in front of it.

"Anna/Nana Kane," went through my mind. She made him open it and when she found it empty, she shot him.

Holmes seemed to have read my thoughts.

"Does it not strike you as strange, Watson, that a woman will take endless trouble over her *toilette*, so that when she steps out to face the world she looks the picture of perfection? Yet, invariably what she leaves behind her in her dressing room is another picture—one of sheer devastation. One of these days you must explain that phenomenon to me, old fellow. Ah, here is Mr. Grandhomme."

I explained to Petit what I wished to achieve and what an odd sight we must have made as we struggled to move that safe off its concrete base. Petit straining his whole diminutive body and me with my one arm. I had almost given up, when inch by inch I felt it begin to slide. With one final effort it began to tip and, finally, its own momentum caused it to fall on to its back, its mouth agape, looking as exhausted as we both felt.

There, in the center of the concrete, was the outline of a small trap door with a ring pull set flush into it. Before I could stop him or say a word, Petit had it in both hands and was pulling it back towards him, a magician demonstrating his crowning trick.

I could feel myself holding my breath as a golden glow started to rise from the depths of that cavity and it would not have surprised me if a live phoenix had slowly flapped its wings in flight and soared over our heads.

Instead I knelt and reached down with my left hand to retrieve the object that had caused the violent death of so many people.

Nicky had chosen to enshroud *his* Bird to protect it from prying eyes. Mallory, having got it, preferred to flaunt his. He had even had the conceit of having the Bird sit on a nest of gold lamé, so that it appeared to be rising from the lick of flames. The man had had a certain taste—a little outre, perhaps, but taste, nonetheless.

I held it up to the light coming into the workroom from the skylight and the ruby eyes seemed to glare right through me. "So who are *you?*" they asked, "and how dare you invade my privacy?"

"I wouldn't get too close, Watson," Holmes said warningly. "Remember, the Bird's kiss is supposed to spell death. A fanciful description, I dare say, but clearly not without some foundation. I see a box over on the counter that should serve as a cage for the last part of our journey."

"And where does that take us, Holmes?" I said aloud and much to Petit's surprise.

"Why, back to where we came in, old fellow. To Osgood Kane's."

I have always believed in the *genius loci*— the spirit of the place—and the *genius* of Kane Towers was distinctly pissed off this morning.

Although the place was stiff with moving bodies, the house itself had a For Sale feel about it. Somebody was making sure all the physical pieces were in place but the house knew. It was simply going through the motions and holding its breath until the moving men came by.

Today I left Mike in the car. The visit would not be of prolonged duration and, besides, he's very sensitive to atmosphere.

The Jeeves character was doing door duty again but even he seemed to have lost some of his previous luster. The previously taut waistcoat seemed distinctly baggy today, as though someone had let some of the air out of him. I suppose to lose *both* ladies of the house in one fell swoop—the one by the hand of the other—

and then have the Master returned like a sack of rotting potatoes is not exactly designed to boost staff morale.

This time we were taken by the short route. On the corner of the stairs we passed the portrait of the young Kane, caught in a random ray of sunlight that—now that I knew the man's background—seemed to create some sort of wishful statement about the glorification of the Aryan race.

What was left of Kane was arranged once more in the Aviary. There was the wheelchair in its preordained place. There were the flocks of birds, wheeling, shrieking and generally doing what birds are destined to do. And there was Kane, propped up with pillows, the eyes dull and the claws of hands still on the arm rests. A slight twitch on the good side of his face was the only sign that he was aware of my presence.

No sophisticated patter today. I hoped that everything Osgood Kane had to say had already been said, because there were no more words where they came from—just a few mewling sounds that meant nothing.

Slowly he inched his head round to face me and I saw something in his eyes that gave me the shivers. It was fear. Not an emotion he had had much to do with, I fancied. And then I realized why. The essence of Osgood Kane was still there, trapped in this treacherous carcass that now frustrated his simplest desires. It was a fitting punishment for someone who had treated the lives of others so lightly and I hoped it would continue long enough for him to learn at least that lesson.

We looked at one another for a long moment. I had little enough to say and he had nothing. Which suited me just fine.

I took the Borgia Bird from its box and placed it in his hand, wrapping the fingers around it, so that it wouldn't fall. Then I stepped back and looked at this pathetic tableau.

So this is what it had all been about. A vicious old man and a chunk of malignant metal. They deserved each other. Now they could have each other.

"And that, Mr. Kane, concludes our business. Have a good life!"

And with that, I turned on my heel and made for the door, where Holmes was already waiting. Behind me, I heard what I could have sworn was a liquid crooning sound.

"Elegantly handled, Watson," said Holmes. Then, as I was about to open the double doors, he raised a hand, indicating that I should wait for a moment more. From where we stood we could no longer see Kane, merely hear the subhuman noises he was making over his prodigal Bird.

But suddenly the noise changed dramatically. The crooning turned into a high-pitched screech that came from no bird ever seen on land or sea. On it went and on and the rest of the birds fell silent.

"The Kiss of death, I fancy, old fellow. You remember our Chinese friend told you of the Bird's secret mechanism? It would seem that Kane now knows that secret but I'm afraid that—like its previous owners—he will not be passing it on.

"And now I think we may take our leave . . ."

The cacophony of the birds resumed as if on cue. In the midst of death life goes on in their world.

The butler was not in attendance as we closed the outer door behind us. Perhaps he had not heard the passing of Osgood Kane. Perhaps he had simply not wanted to acknowledge it. Perhaps he was busy polishing up his résumé. In any event, Holmes and I were free to stroll back down those cheerless corridors.

Now that it was all over, I was frankly feeling a little down. I suppose I had solved the case—with more than a little help from Holmes—but the cost in terms of human life and happiness weighed upon me. Perhaps taxidermy *would* be a suitable alternative occupation after all. At least your clients started *out* dead!

Holmes seemed to read my mood.

"I know how you feel, old fellow. Once or twice in my career I feel I may have done more real harm by my discovery of the criminal than ever he had done by his crime. But that is not true in this case. You have helped achieve something the law would have failed to do. You have brought about that little thing called—Justice."

There was to be one more postscript that will not go into my account, should I ever write it.

We were passing Kane's portrait once more, when Holmes stopped for some reason and moved up close to it. Then I saw him frame the face with his hands, obliterating the rest of the body and background. Even though his own body was insubstantial, it still served to crop the picture, so that only the center of the face was now visible.

"My eyes have been trained to examine faces and not their trimmings," I heard him say.

"Oh, my God!" I heard myself say.

I was looking at the face of Nicky Parmentieri!

"A Greek tragedy, Watson. I do declare, a veritable Greek tragedy. Nicky was clearly the other twin. Kane dispatched him and put the child out of his mind. He no longer existed. The last thing he expected was that the boy should acquire another and even more deadly family and then come back to plague him—in total ignorance, of course, about his own parentage.

"Then—confusion worse confounded—brother and sister meet and feel the strong empathy that often exists between twin siblings. Not knowing that they are, in fact, committing incest, they become lovers. Perhaps Nana in her already disturbed mental state begins to have some premonition that something is wrong but Nicky certainly does not. He takes his pleasures lightly and wherever he can find them. His true father's true son. He moves on to his surrogate mother. I tell you, Watson, if Euripides had ever devised such a plot, it would have transformed classical theatre.

"And then the Eumenides arrive—in the shape of Watson and Holmes—summoned up by Kane of all people. And thus the tragic outcome we have just witnessed became inevitable. Pity and terror, old fellow. The Unities. Catharsis."

It took a few moments for it all to sink in and then I said—

"The only consolation, Holmes, is that none of them *knew* what they had done."

"I imagine you have observed, Watson, the plethora of gardeners Mr. Kane has working on his property this morning? The fact that they appear without exception to be of an Oriental persuasion is surely a tribute to the horticultural skills of that ingenious race."

EPILOGUE

We were driving along with the top of the Corvette down to take advantage of the late sun.

Mike was leaning out to scrutinize passers-by for criminal tendencies.

I was letting my mind go into neutral as I turned over the events of the last few days. What should I have done differently? What might I have done better? How could I have done *any* of it without the shadowy man at my side? And why was I more and more beginning to feel that there was something in Holmes's insistence that all of this had happened before in some other time and place that was becoming increasingly real to me? That was a three Jack Daniel's problem for another time.

I turned to say so to Holmes and found to my surprise that he looked more ectoplasmic than usual. To be perfectly honest, he was fading before my eyes. Seeing my surprise and concern, he leaned across and would have touched my arm, if he could.

"Old fellow, something tells me that my time here is run. I sense that I am needed elsewhere." Then, seeing my obvious distress—"But never fear, that same something tells me that neither time nor space shall ever quite separate the old firm. I hope I have been of some help. And as for you, Watson, I never cease to learn from you.

"If you ever need me, Watson, all you have to do is whistle. You know how to whistle, don't you? You put your lips together—and blow."

"But Holmes," I cried, "that's what Bacall says to Bogart in *To Have and Have Not*. How did you . . . ?"

But I was alone in the Corvette, except for Mike in the shotgun seat, who was baying at the sky.

THE BEGINNING . . .

Center Point Large Print
600 Brooks Road / PO Box 1
Thorndike, ME 04986-0001 USA

(207) 568-3717

**US & Canada:
1 800 929-9108
www.centerpointlargeprint.com**